Soul's Temptation

Soul's Temptation

Navi' Robins

www.urbanbooks.net

Urban Books, LLC
300 Farmingdale Road, NY-Route 109
Farmingdale, NY 11735

ISBN 13: 978-1-64556-192-7
ISBN 10: 1-64556-192-5

First Trade Paperback Printing April 2021
Printed in the United States of America

10 9 8 7 6 5 4 3 2 1

Distributed by Kensington Publishing Corp.
Submit Orders to:
Customer Service
400 Hahn Road
Westminster, MD 21157-4627
Phone: 1-800-733-3000
Fax: 1-800-659-2436

Soul's Temptation

by

Navi' Robins

Chapter One

The Contract

A hell's fire . . . The burning in his chest felt like a dark magician had conjured the bottomless pit of hell in his lungs, and the pain was unbearable. However, nothing burned more than having to look at the blue-eyed assassin loom over him, watching in the darkness with a look of intense satisfaction as he died painfully from the lethal injection they administered. His mouth opened and closed like a giant catfish out of the water, trying to breathe, and each time he inhaled, death drew closer. As the neurotoxins moved through his veins, clotting his blood, and shutting down his respiratory system, the ultra-attractive, blue-eyed assassin periodically checked their watch. As his large body started to shake, the assassin braced all their weight on the man's chest, preventing him from getting up from his king-size bed. Suddenly, the man began to convulse and bounce violently on the bed, his body making one last attempt at surviving before the cobra's venom took its toll.

Now, the man's eyes began to bleed out, and his lips turned pale as he took his last breath. The assassin carefully examined the man's body while checking for a pulse. After a few seconds, the assassin cautiously picked up a black bag from the floor. The bag immediately began to twist and hiss as the king cobra inside tried to fight itself free from the murderer's grip. Observing the bag vigilantly, the killer watched the bag move, calculating where the cobra's head and tail were. Then clutching the bag with both hands and twisting it brutally, the assassin snapped the cobra's back in two. The cobra began to violently thrash around in the bag as the assassin turned the bag upside down and watched the wounded cobra fall on top of the still body.

The cobra's reflexes went into overdrive as it repeatedly sank its teeth deep into the body's flesh, injecting massive amounts of poison into the corpse. Satisfied that the mission was accomplished, the assassin slowly backed away into the shadows and disappeared . . .

Four hours later
Cairo, Egypt

John Smith stood on the roof of the Four Seasons Hotel Cairo, taking in the majesty of the Nile River as its pristine waters reflected the Egyptian sunrise over the horizon. As he admired the sunlight licking the top of Cairo's impressive city skyline, he felt a sudden vibration in his inner left blazer pocket. Without looking at the screen on his phone, he placed the phone to his ear and said, "Speak."

"Father is requesting your presence in the field."

"I've just finished a harvest. Get someone else to do it."

"Father doesn't trust anyone else to handle this harvest. Father feels your previous experience with this crop will prove most useful."

A confused look erupted on John's face right before he responded, "There's no such thing as previous experiences with harvests. They are either harvested, or they're not."

"That wasn't a harvest. It was a survey of the fields to persuade the plants to grow in the direction that Father found profitable."

John immediately understood who and what was being asked of him, and he sighed while rolling his eyes at the idea of having to revisit a previous assignment. He'd given his word they would be left alone, and he always kept his word.

"Father gave the assurance that the crop in question wouldn't be harvested if it was compliant."

"There's been another development that could drastically deplete Father's yearly profits if this crop is allowed to grow."

"I gave my word. I'm sure Father understands what that means to a man in my profession. With all of Father's influence, he should've seen or anticipated this new development coming and instructed me to refrain from giving my word that the crop would be allowed to grow without interference. At this juncture, I am unable to take this assignment. He's going to have to get another farmer to harvest this crop."

A long silence followed as the man on the other end of the phone contemplated his response to John's refusal of the contract. Thirty seconds later, that man cleared his throat and responded, "Father doesn't care about keeping your word. Father only cares about your loyalty, but I will inform Father of your decision as you wish. A stern word of advice: stay clear of this harvest. If Father finds out of your interference in any capacity . . . the harvester will become the harvested."

Rolling his eyes, John abruptly ended the call and threw his phone like an outfielder aiming for home plate. Gritting his teeth, he looked down at the ground and kicked the gravel covering the roof of the five-star hotel. Sighing forcefully, he looked up at the sky, contemplating if it would have been better to accept the contract instead of allowing someone else to break the promise he made to the Bennetts.

Chapter Two

They're Still at It

Twelve hours later
Chicago, Illinois

A quiet hiss escaped her lips as he pulled her blond hair, snatching her head back. She suddenly felt his warm and wet tongue passionately move up and down her neck, the sensation causing her entire body to tremble with pleasure. Biting her neck, he pressed himself against her ass and began to grind on her slowly. A loud moan escaped her lips as she felt his hard, thick, and warm ten-inch rod move between her cheeks. The anticipation of him ravaging her body drove her insane. Pushing her head against the wall in front of her, he leaned backward and smacked her on the ass, her peach-colored skin turning red from the contact. His condo's front door was wide open, allowing the cool night breeze to invade the large entryway into his home, causing her nipples to swell and tingle.

Lifting her arms above her head, Timothy ran his tongue down the back of her neck and slowly down to the small of her back until he reached the top of her ample backside. Spreading her butt cheeks apart, he inhaled deeply and plunged his entire head between her assets.

The sudden sensation of his warm tongue exploring her forbidden parts caused her to scratch and claw at the wall as she leaned forward, allowing him more access to her.

Oh my God, what is he doing to me?

As he continued to devour her, Meagan began to feel the building heat and vibrations announcing the coming of an orgasm so intense that someone would need a mop to clean up its aftermath on the black marble floor in the foyer.

"Oh, shit, baby, I'm coming; don't stop. Please, don't stop. Keep eating that pussy. Oh yes! Fuck me with your tongue . . . mmm . . . Yes, that's it. Suck that clit . . . aaah . . . shit."

She suddenly felt her inner tunnel tighten and the roaring rapids of her orgasm rushing out of her. Her eyes rolled back into her head as her mouth flung open, and her body shook as if a bolt of lightning just struck her.

I'm really gonna fuck her ass up now.

Without warning, the man reached forward, gently spread her lotus lips, and began massaging her clitoris in a circular motion. The sudden sensation made her scream and tumble backward. As her body went limp, he braced her against his thighs, holding her against the wall. Bending her over, he slowly got down on the floor while pulling her down with him. Still holding her by her hips, he pulled her down and guided her onto his waiting and throbbing muscle in one fluid motion. As soon as she felt him slide inside of her, she leaned forward, digging her nails into his legs, attempting to brace herself for the pleasure and pain of his size and girth. Shaking and shrieking, she began to bounce while moving her hips like an exotic dancer, and he watched her in curious amazement.

"Gad damn! Look at that ass bounce. Take this dick. Take it, take it, take it, take it. Oh, fuck. This shit is good, ain't it?"

Trying to contain the scream dancing on her tongue, she bit down on her bottom lip and whispered, "Mmm-hmmm." Within a few minutes, she felt another climax building as his muscles tensed up, his legs began to tremble, and his toes started to curl.

Mmm . . . Yes, he's coming, she thought, right before she jumped up, spun around, and shoved all of him in her mouth. She immediately closed her mouth around him while making wavelike motions on the underside of his shaft. A roar erupted from his lips as he released a massive load of his essence inside her mouth. As she felt his warm nectar fill her mouth, she closed her eyes while moaning deeply, allowing the vibrations to add to the sensation of her sucking him while he climaxed.

Feeling his self-control peel away, he started twisting his body to the side, attempting to remove himself from her mouth, but each time he tried, she locked her jaws tighter around him while being careful not to let her teeth scrape him.

Panting and slamming his hand down on the floor, he quickly accepted he wasn't going to shake her, so he braced himself as his explosion continued longer than he'd thought possible. Noticing he was done, she slowly lifted her mouth from his shaft while making sure not to leave a drop of his essence behind. Smiling, she stood up and strolled into the hallway bathroom.

After a few seconds, the toilet flushed, and the bathroom sink faucet started to run as she reached into the medicine cabinet, pulling out her toothbrush, and began brushing her teeth. Still lying on the floor in complete awe, he turned his attention to the wide-open front door and smiled. He knew his nosy neighbors heard the commotion and probably attempted to sneak a peek, but he didn't care. Meagan was incredible and worth the trouble of a fine from the condo association. So, if she wanted to keep the door open, that's exactly what Timothy did. He'd rarely met a woman like Meagan, and he did everything he could to show her exactly how much he cherished her body and mind.

Meagan walked out of the bathroom, smiling while watching Timothy tremble on the floor. Suddenly, a cold draft blew up her sweaty back. Shaking, she turned and noticed the open door and quickly closed it.

Timothy sat up and watched Meagan stroll toward him and asked, "No swallowing, huh?"

Shaking her head, she responded, "Nope, but I dropped your kids off at the pool. Besides, swallowing means that I love you, and we both know that's not what either of us wants, so . . ."

No, that's not what you *want,* Timothy thought as he stood to his feet.

"Anyway, babes, I gotta go. You really relaxed me. Thank you." Then reaching down and touching herself, she said, "Lucy definitely thanks you. She really needed that. How long it's been?"

"Three long months," Timothy responded coldly.

Looking at him like a cute pet, Meagan reached out and ran her hand along his cheek.

"So, you're actually leaving *right now?*"

"Yes, I am. I have to go see Ayana, and what I have to tell her is gonna be devastating, but I have to tell her."

"What is it?"

"What is what?"

"What you have to tell Ayana?"

Exhaling, Meagan responded, "President Ibrahim Bassa Alraheem is dead."

"Huh . . . how . . . how . . . how did he . . .?" he stammered while placing his hand on his forehead.

"Snakebite. Actually, it was a king cobra. They say it put enough venom into him to kill an elephant. Fortunately, the man was so strong he killed the snake before his untimely death created another conflict in South Sudan, which is the last thing they need right now. That man was just . . . amazing. He was a great leader, and I know Ayana had such high hopes for her country under his leadership. The vice president isn't such a bad guy either, but with another election coming up in a little under a year, things could turn out dreadful if the wrong person were elected to office, like that Thomas Bossa."

Without warning, he suddenly felt light-headed, and the room started to spin. Stumbling, he quickly braced himself against the wall behind him. Noticing his reaction, Meagan rushed over, trying to stop him from tumbling to the floor. Searching his eyes, she asked, "Babe, what's wrong?"

Looking up at the ceiling while trying to regain his balance, he nodded slowly. Then letting out a quick chuckle, he responded, "I think I must've come so hard, I got dizzy or something. Woman, you're trying to kill me or something?"

Giving him the side eye, Meagan flashed a sarcastic smirk while watching him walk over to the living room and flop down on the oversized, dark brown leather couch.

He's just going to sit bare ass on the leather, I see, she thought while turning up her nose. *Note to self: never lie face down on that couch again.*

Forcing a smile, although she felt nauseated, she asked, "Babe, are you sure you're okay?"

"Yeah, yeah, I'm good," he responded while waving his hand in her direction. "Go ahead and get ready to go see Ayana."

"Are you sure? Just a minute ago you weren't too happy abou—"

"Yeah, I was tripping," he said, cutting her off. "Get ready. I'll be fine."

Meagan stared at Timothy for a few seconds longer before she shrugged, snatched up her overnight bag, and rushed into the bathroom to get ready.

Two hours later
Highland Park, Illinois

The reflection in the mirror made Ayana's stomach churn as she turned from right to left, praying there was an angle that could hide this new yet downgraded body of hers. She placed her hand over her womb and stared at the many stretch marks that lined her belly. A smile grew on her face when she noticed the shea butter cream was working to remove them, but she still had a long way to go. Turning to the side again, she sighed while shaking her head at her stomach and excess fat that lined her hips and inner thighs. She'd vowed to herself that after she was able to move around on her own, she would work off the baby fat. However, life sometimes has a different plan, and after two years of being a stay-at-home mother, she hadn't done one push-up or run a single mile. In her defense, Li'l Timothy was an energetic and curious child, and she always chased after him around the house, trying to prevent him from getting into everything he had no business getting into.

Daniel promised her that he would help with Timothy's care, but after his book became an international phenomenon, he couldn't keep his promise. His sudden literary fame, paired with his obsession with training, made him a ghost around the house. Even when he was home, he wasn't home. The very thought of it caused her nose to flare as her anger began to build.

Suddenly, she noticed how gravity and the lack of exercise affected her breasts, and she whimpered as her eyes began to water. Feeling hopeless, she threw her hands up and stormed out of her massive closet, deciding she'd had enough and should take the opportunity to get ready while Timothy was napping.

An hour later, Ayana answered her doorbell, and, at the sight of Meagan, she leaped into her arms, and the two friends embraced for over a minute. Meagan's eyes widened as she took in their massive mansion, and by the time the two women were seated in the family room, Meagan was highly impressed.

"Wow, Ayana, you have a beautiful home," Meagan proclaimed while looking around with admiration. "Definitely a huge upgrade from that downtown penthouse."

"Thank you. Yes, it is," Ayana replied, smiling while looking around and reminding herself just how much her life has changed since the day she walked into Daniel's office.

"How are things, girl? I see you've settled into the housewife life," Meagan teased while playfully shoving Ayana's shoulder.

Desperate housewife is more like it. Save me, Meagan, Ayana thought while forcing a smile so exaggerated that it alarmed Meagan. She knew Ayana better than anyone, and she knew something was wrong. So, she reached out, held her hand, and said, "Ayana, talk to me."

"I'm not used to this life, Meagan. A stay-at-home mom who's barely holding it together and gaining more weight every day," Ayana complained while looking down at her midsection.

"Girl, you're not fat. You look great."

Ayana's head shot up, flashing Meagan a look that chilled Meagan's blood. Feeling uncomfortable, she quickly responded, "Okay, maybe you've gained a little weight, but you still look better than most of the women that have had a baby."

"I'm sure, but I don't feel like myself anymore. I feel lost and spread out all over the place. Don't get me wrong. I love my life, my husband, and I love Timothy with all my heart and soul, but I feel like I don't know what I'm supposed to do now that I'm a mother."

"Have you talked to Danny about how you feel?"

Ayana rolled her eyes and sucked her teeth at the very idea of Danny listening to her. The longer she thought about his absence, she suddenly didn't want to be touched, so she snatched her hand away from Meagan.

"Ooh, that can't be good."

"He's never home. I know he's a celebrity and everything, but I thought that after he became a multimillionaire from his book sales and didn't have to work at the hospital, we would have more time together. But he's either traveling somewhere for another interview, or he's at that fucking training facility."

"Training facility?"

"Yeah, ever since he came in contact with you know who, he's been obsessed with training and learning how to fight and protect us, just in case he returns."

"Ayana, you have to understand that until that time, Danny didn't know men like that existed. Once you run into those kinds of people, most respond by running and hiding or preparing yourself. Danny isn't a runner, so he's trying to do what he has to do to keep his family safe."

"But he needs to be home to do that, right? How can he protect us if he's never where we are?"

Nodding, Meagan said, "You make a great point."

Ayana sighed forcefully, folded her arms, and lay back on the couch. Meagan looked at her and then looked away. She had no idea her friend was such an emotional mess, and she wondered if now was the best time to break the bad news to her. Suddenly, a confused look came over her face, and she started looking around.

"Girl, where's Li'l Timmy?"

"He's taking a nap."

Inhaling deeply, Meagan tapped Ayana on her leg, and Ayana sat up, and when she looked into Meagan's eyes, she knew something was terribly wrong.

"What's going on, Meagan?"

"Ayana, I'm so sorry. I hate to add more stress to you, but your friend President Alraheem is dead."

Ayana screamed and covered her mouth as tears welled in her eyes. Frantically, she began looking around as if someone were calling out to her, and her body shook as tears ran down her face. Trying to console her, Meagan reached out to hold her, but Ayana jumped up from the couch and walked over to the large fireplace, turning her back to Meagan. Meagan sat on the sofa, listening to Ayana moan in agony until it began to move her to tears. Meagan wanted to join her friend by the fireplace and hold her in her arms, but she knew Ayana needed to mourn her friend in solitude. After crying until her head ached, Ayana aggressively wiped the tears from her eyes, turned around, and asked, "Who killed him?"

Oh shit, Meagan thought, right before she jumped up from the couch, waving her hands in the air. After experiencing Ayana backtracking to her days as the unwilling wife of a warlord, the last thing Meagan needed was for her friend to pick up another assault rifle and go looking for a killer that didn't exist.

"Wait, Ayana! No one killed him. A cobra got inside his room and attacked him while he was asleep. The poison and the president's weight contributed to his death. He was not murdered."

"A cobra?" Ayana asked with a look of disbelief.

"Yes, it was just a cobra. Nothing more."

"If that's the case, can you explain how a cobra got to the third floor of a heavily guarded building and didn't bite anyone else before reaching the president's room? There's too much traffic at the palace for that snake to make its way up to his room and not be noticed."

"Ayana, the doctor's confirmed he died from snake's venom."

"Yes, but, Meagan, you of all people should know that no president's death is that innocent or cut and dry. Would you believe a snake killed your president in the White House?"

"No . . . huh . . . no . . . why would he . . . I don't understand the question, Ayana," Meagan stammered while shaking her head, trying to understand what Ayana was saying.

"My point exactly. Just because my president lives in Africa doesn't mean death by a snake bite is an acceptable excuse. Someone murdered my friend and tried to cover it up. I need to get home at once."

"Ayana, you *are* home. You can't allow your need to feel important to cloud your judgment. Timmy needs you here, not back in Sudan."

"If you think I'm going to let them murder my friend and president and get away with it, you have me fucked up, Meagan."

"The last time you were over there trying to save the world, you ended up in a coma for almost two years. If what you're saying is true, and Alraheem was murdered, that means you are diving right back into the frying pan with some people that are more ruthless and powerful than Kronte—especially if they can murder a head of state and cover it up. We are talking about people like the ones your husband has been training for. Going against those kinds of individuals usually doesn't work in your favor. You can rest assured, Daniel will follow you over there, and the two of you could be killed, leaving Li'l Timothy with whom? Your in-laws? Timothy?"

Without warning, Ayana began screaming at the top of her lungs and then collapsed to her knees. Meagan jumped back and almost fell over the coffee table when Ayana's piercing scream filled her ears. Ayana started rocking back and forth, trying to calm the rage building up inside of her. She wanted to uncover the assassination of her country's president, and if this had happened four years ago, then she would've dismissed Meagan's warning and went to war. Today, however, she had more to lose than she ever had in her entire life, which rendered her powerless to do anything about it. She knew with this new covert attack on her homeland that it was only a matter of time before the storm of war returned to her country, raining down destruction on her people, more than likely so someone in a suit and tie could profit from the natural resources that were rightfully the inheritance of her people. Ayana looked up at Meagan with a sorrow so deep that it made Meagan's heart skip a beat, and tears immediately began running down her face.

Joining Ayana on her knees, Meagan held both of her hands and said, "I know you will want to be there for his funeral, so I'll make the necessary security arrangements so that you and your family are safe. I know it's not nearly enough, but it's all I can do at the moment."

Suddenly, a tiny voice said, "Mommy, what are you doing?"

The two women quickly jumped to their feet. Meagan stood in front of Ayana, hiding her from her son until she could get herself together. Once Ayana had wiped away her tears, she gently tapped Meagan on the shoulder, and Meagan stepped to the side.

"Nothing, baby. Me and Auntie Meagan were just praying. Are you hungry?"

Li'l Timothy stared at his mother and Meagan with a suspicious look on his face. "But, Mommy, you sound like you've been crying. Did this lady hurt you?"

"This lady?" Meagan gasped, placing her hand on her chest. "Timmy, I'm not Auntie Meagan anymore?"

Timmy's eyebrows slowly lifted while he shook his head and said, "Nope. If you hurt Mommy, you're not my auntie anymore."

"Aww, baby," Ayana said, smacking her lips. "This is Mommy's 'bestest' friend in the whole wide world, and she would never do anything to hurt me. Come and say hi, baby."

Timmy didn't move as he looked at both women, trying to decide if he wanted to say hi. Eventually, he looked at his mother, and the trust he had for her won, and he ran over and embraced Meagan. Meagan was instantly filled with the warmth of love as Timmy wrapped his little arms around her neck.

"Hi, Auntie Meagan, happy to see you again."

"Nice to see you again too, Timmy," Meagan responded, closing her eyes to fight back the tears that were trying to escape down her face. Timmy then planted a warm kiss on her cheek and ran over to his mother, who lifted him in her arms and asked, "Are you hungry, baby?"

"Yes," Timmy responded eagerly.

"What do you want to eat?"

"*Peanub lutter* and jelly."

"*Peanub lutter* and jelly? What's that?"

"Mommy, you know what it is."

"Yes, yes . . . Mommy knows *exactly* what it is. Can Auntie Meagan join us for lunch?"

Timmy looked over at Meagan, smiled, and nodded his head.

"Why, thank you, Timmy. I would be honored to have lunch with you," Meagan responded happily.

"Okay, but you have to eat *allll* your food. Even your vegetables," Timmy replied, waving his finger in the air. "If not, Mommy won't give you a treat . . . Okay?"

"I promise to eat all of my food."

Timmy nodded, and the three of them walked into the kitchen to have lunch and a much-lighter moment after a traumatic afternoon.

Chapter Three

Preparing for the Worst, Investing in the Best

Twenty-four hours later
Highland Park, Illinois

Beads of sweat formed on Daniel's forehead as he strained his ears to locate where the sounds of movement were coming from. The entire place was dark, and turning on the lights could mean whoever was moving in the darkness would be able to locate him long before he could find them. Swallowing hard, he walked along the wall using it as a marker, as well as making sure his back was covered. Using his left hand, he ran it along the wall so that he knew when the wall ended and an empty space began. His fingers suddenly felt the edges of the wall, and he bent down, placing one hand on the floor and his other firmly gripping his handgun. He could hear them moving to his left, but he couldn't pinpoint exactly where they were, and firing blindly into the dark could give the intruder his location, making him an easy target.

Holding his breath, Daniel quickly moved a few feet ahead until his hand felt the edge of another wall. Placing his back against the wall, he began to move along it while listening attentively to the sounds of the intruders.

*I'm almost there. I can hear his heavy breathing,
more than likely accelerated from fear. To my left . . . a
little farther . . . a bit farther. There he is . . .*

Before Daniel could raise his gun in the direction of
the intruder's breathing, he heard a loud pop behind him.
He quickly dove across the floor right before the entire
room erupted in the noisy, piercing sounds of gunfire.
Bullets flew from every direction as the flash of the guns
expelling their arsenal illuminated the room, and Daniel
took a mental note where each intruder was located.
Sliding across the floor on his back, Daniel fired in the
direction of the intruder behind him. The intruder yelled
out in pain as Daniel's bullets found their target multiple
times, and the intruder's gun immediately stopped firing.
Knowing he only had a few more seconds before the
second and third intruder would be firing on his position,
Daniel rolled to the other side of the wall and ducked
behind the corner.

Observing, he noticed just as he anticipated that the
two remaining intruders began firing on his previous
location. Through the flashing lights, he watched one of
the intruders move across his line of sight. Daniel quickly
fired two shots, hitting the intruder in the chest. Yelling
out in pain, the intruder stumbled and collapsed to the
floor. Daniel began moving swiftly around the corner and
over to the far side of the room, flanking the last intruder
on his left. The intruder appeared to be in a panic as
he frantically moved around in the dark and fired his
weapon, hoping a bullet would find the elusive doctor.
The doctor knew he only had a few seconds before the
thought of shooting directly behind him would enter the
intruder's mind. Moving as quickly as his tired legs could
carry him, Daniel zigzagged until he was now behind the
intruder, then suddenly stood up and placed the muzzle
of his gun on the back of the intruder's head.

"*Bang,* you're dead!" Daniel laughed loudly and suddenly. The entire room lit up as the sound of a bullhorn echoed throughout the training facility. A large group of people moved into the training room, applauding Daniel's accomplishment of finally passing the course.

"Doctor Bennett, for a saver of lives, you are more ruthless than any of my other trainees."

Smiling while he quickly unloaded the gun's magazine filled with rubber-tipped bullets, Daniel responded, "The ER can be a dangerous place at times, Lieutenant Commander."

"I'm sure," Lieutenant Commander Ruiz replied while giving Daniel a congratulatory pat on the shoulder. "You're a natural, Doctor. Probably, one of my most talented trainees. I'm just hoping everything you've learned here over the last three years will help you protect your family."

Nodding in agreement, Daniel responded, "I'm sure it will help tremendously."

The lieutenant then looked behind Daniel and noticed an anxious Timothy standing in the doorway of the training facility. Sniffing and shaking his head, the lieutenant gestured for Daniel to look behind him, and when Daniel turned around, he quickly noticed that Timothy looked as if he'd been through hell.

"Congratulations again, Doctor. We're gonna miss you here, but you're always welcome back anytime you want. Just leave 'Magic Doctor Juan' at home."

Daniel remained silent as his eyebrows lifted as high as they could go, and his full lips retreated inside his mouth. Daniel hated that after Timothy was caught having sex in the bathroom of the training facility with one of the female trainees, who was also the lieutenant's girlfriend, he had to be reminded of it every day. Noticing Daniel's reaction, Ruiz walked away. Sighing while shaking his head, Daniel walked over to Timothy, and the closer he got to him, the more out of sorts he appeared.

"Let me guess . . . Meagan's in town?" Daniel asked while trying to look as serious as he could. But despite his best efforts, a smile slowly grew on his face.

"No . . . wait . . . Yeah, she is . . . but that's not why I'm here," Timothy stammered while glaring at the rage-inducing smile on Daniel's face.

"Really? Because I remember distinctly Lieutenant Ruiz banning you from the facility after you and Deborah decided it couldn't wait. So, if you're not here to tell me how Meagan left you limp and leaking again, I'm really confused about why you're standing inside this building."

Timothy opened his mouth to speak but was abruptly interrupted by a light-skinned beauty that flung her arms around Daniel's neck and planted a kiss on his cheek. She hung onto his neck as if her life depended on it, allowing her kiss to last much longer than the typical platonic greeting. Timothy looked her over and noticed through the camouflage pants, with more pockets than a South Side alleyway, her ass seemed to jump out at him. The rest of her body was equally impressive, and as she embraced Daniel, her breasts appeared to spill over the sides of her shirt. To say she was impressive was an understatement, and typically, Timothy would be aroused, seeing such a physically gifted woman. But the way she hung on his friend made him uncomfortable and upset at the same time.

"Oh my God, Danny, I'm so happy for you. The way you took out those guys without taking any damage was just fucking awesome and sexy too. I'm kind of sad you'll be leaving us, but I hope you come to visit sometime."

Daniel noticed Timothy's suspicious look and tried to pry her away from him, but she hung on tighter until Timothy cleared his throat, startling her. Jumping, she turned around and squealed loudly before extending her hand and said, "Hi, my name is Cloe LaRue," she said gleefully. Timothy found himself mesmerized by the unusual yet captivating blue color of her eyes, especially for an African American woman. He looked down at her hand with his nose turned up, and after several seconds had decided he didn't want to touch her. Pushing her hand out of the way and staring at Daniel as if he'd lost his mind, Timothy moved past her as if she didn't exist. Cloe's bright smile instantly evaporated, and the sunshine quickly turned to clouds as she shuffled her feet and hurried away in embarrassment.

"What?" Daniel asked while pretending there was something of importance in his military vest pockets that he needed.

"Don't fucking play with me. Who is the young and dumb redbone?"

"Who, Cloe? She's a new trainee here. She started a few months ago. She can be a little touchy-feely, but she's very talented."

"Yeah, I'm sure she has all kinds of talents," Timothy responded while looking in the direction where Cloe just fled. "Have you lost your mind? You *do* know your wife used to train and run with guerilla soldiers in South Sudan, right? She will castrate you and definitely do things to Cloe that would make Kronte seem like a shoo-in for the Nobel Prize."

"Tim, it's not like that. She's just a friend. That's all."

"I'm not married, and even *I* know no married man should have female friends that look like Cloe."

"Ayana trusts me. She knows I love her and would never do anything to hurt her."

"Really? So, has she met Cloe?"

"No, she ha—"

"Exactly! Shut the fuck up, and let's get out of here. We need to talk, and I don't want to discuss this around these crazy people."

"These people aren't crazy. They're just concerned about protecting their families in case they are faced with a well-trained threat."

Breathing forcefully while smacking himself on his forehead, Timothy responded, "Oh, my bad. They're not crazy. They're just concerned citizens that need to pay thousands of dollars to an ex-Navy SEAL commander to learn how to fight, shoot, and be proficient in counterterrorism tactics. Things they'll *definitely* need shortly."

"Some of us have already faced highly trained threats," Daniel snapped back while taking a step closer to Timothy.

Not intimidated by Daniel's aggression, Timothy chuckled and responded while pushing Daniel away from him. "You *actually* think three years here will prepare you for a highly skilled and cold-blooded assassin like John Sm—"

"Shut your mouth," Daniel growled. "This is *not* the place to discuss that man."

Tapping Daniel on the chest playfully, Timothy replied, "You know what, Sambo . . . I mean, Rambo . . . You're right. This ain't the place, so shall we leave, or would you like me to use the restroom again? I feel like I need to release some tension, and Cloe looks *willing* and definitely *able*."

Daniel stared at Timothy, gritting his teeth and lowering his eyelids until they were almost closed. Amused by Daniel's angry stare, Timothy responded with an antagonizing smirk. He then stepped aside and gestured for Daniel to walk ahead of him.

"After you," he said while bowing slightly like a butler. Right before Timothy walked out of doors, he yelled out, "Make way; dead man walking."

***

"Where are we going?" Daniel nervously asked once he noticed Timothy walking away from the training facility's parking lot.

"Just follow me. I know you're not nervous, are you? I mean, with all that training you have, you should be strutting your stuff like you have zero fucks to give."

"Even a trained man wants to know where the fuck he's going."

"Just keep walking, and you'll see."

Shaking his head, Daniel continued to follow Timothy through downtown Highland Park, which looked as if it were cut out of a holiday catalog. The northern suburb was festively decorated in red, brown, black, and orange for the upcoming Halloween and fall season. Looking around, Daniel tried to make sure the two men weren't being followed, but it seemed that everyone was oblivious to the two of them walking fast down the streets of this wealthy Chicago suburb. They finally walked into the Highland Park Metra Train Station, and Timothy quickly boarded the train. Daniel paused for a few seconds while he surveyed his surroundings. Once he was satisfied they weren't followed, he climbed aboard the train. Looking down the train's long aisle and then up at the seats on the second level, he located Timothy sitting across from an empty seat.

What is going on with this fool? Daniel thought as he made his way to the second level. Seated in the chair across from Timothy, Daniel gestured for Timothy to explain what was going on. Timothy raised his hand in the air and looked out the window. Shaking his head, Daniel sat back in his seat and waited for Timothy to come out of his cloak-and-dagger fantasy. Within a couple of minutes, the train began to move, and Timothy leaned forward and began speaking in a lowered and frightened tone.

"I did it."

Daniel's eyebrows slanted to the middle of his eyes as he asked, "Did what?"

Timothy just gave Daniel a very confident look and nodded.

"Oh shit! You found the cur—"

"Shut the fuck up!" Timothy said while looking around to make sure no one heard Daniel's outburst.

Confused, Daniel shook his head while giving Timothy the side eye.

"Dude, why are you acting like this isn't the best news to ever happen in recent human history?"

Timothy remained silent and looked away toward the window, watching the landscape roll by. His eyes started to water as he reflected on the consequences of his lack of judgment and the millions of people adversely affected by it. He knew no matter who he went to, there was a level of danger to come along with it, but he felt things could've been different had he considered the events that unfolded three years ago. Knowing they didn't have much time on the train before it became crowded with inner-city commuters, Timothy leaned closer to Daniel and responded, "Because I believe some very powerful people are watching me and don't want this . . . you know . . . to get out. I think that's why my previous investor . . . backed out."

"Wait. How long have you known about what you have?" Daniel whispered while trying to hold in his anger that his best friend had confided in someone else before he trusted in him.

"It's been about three months. I immediately reached out to someone who had the capital and the character to do right by this miracle. The thing is that it's not just a cure but also a vaccine. Zero side effects and once taken, the host is forever immune to the disease and any derivative it may have."

Daniel's eyes widened as he slowly sat back in his chair, placing his hand over his mouth. Looking up at the plain cream ceiling of the train, Daniel shook his head and smiled. Although he should be furious with Timothy, he was filled with pride that his best friend was about to save the world. Blowing forcefully, Daniel asked, "What can I do to help?"

"I need investors. Correction, I need *discreet* investors to keep this thing under wraps until I have perfected an inexpensive method of mass-producing it. The investment would pay off huge, and I do mean *huge*. Although I plan on selling it at a price that will be cheap and affordable for everyone, there will still be a huge profit made."

"How much do you need?"

"Right now, my early estimates range from two hundred to four hundred and fifty million dollars. That will cover a new secure lab, a workforce of about four hundred, production, and distribution. I'm anticipating twelve months from initial setup to when the first batch of the vaccine will be distributed to countries that suffer the most from the disease, and then a new batch will follow every three months. Investors' return is estimated at around 10,000 percent at least."

"My God! This *is* real, isn't it?" Daniel asked as a cold chill ran through his body. "Brother, you know I got your back. Although I don't have anywhere near four hundred and fifty million dollars to invest, I do have sixty million I will gladly give you to get the ball rolling."

Shocked, Timothy responded, "That's a lot of money, Danny. Even for you, that's almost your entire net worth."

"Not quite. It is a large chunk of it, but how could I say no to my best friend and godfather to my son? How could I say no to saving the world?"

"Don't forget about that 10,000 percent return."

"Well, that would definitely sweeten the investment," Daniel chuckled awkwardly. "But I feel like there's more to this than just an investor backing out. I won't push because I can tell this discovery is a much-bigger burden than you anticipated when you first started on this journey, bro. But you don't have to deal with this alone, and besides investing, I'm willing to do whatever you need to make this dream a reality."

Timothy looked over at Daniel with eyes filled with regret, unable to bring himself to tell his best friend everything. However, he knew his life could be in danger, so he inhaled deeply and responded, "I have to be honest with you, Danny. My last investor didn't back out . . . willingly. He's dead, and I have an eerie feeling that his commitment to this project was the reason for his untimely death."

Daniel's head jerked back as he listened to Timothy's explanation. Suddenly, all of Timothy's strange behavior started to make sense.

"Who was the investor?"

"President Alraheem," Timothy responded right before covering his eyes and collapsing back in his seat in exhaustion.

Daniel's eyes widened until they began to hurt. His heart rate accelerated as he started to feel dizzy. Looking down at the floor, he contemplated everything that Ayana had shared with him the night before, after Meagan's visit. All of her suspicions he felt were outlandish at the time, which caused them to argue the entire evening. Daniel had agreed with Meagan that Ayana was looking for a reason to throw herself back into the fray. Ayana made some crucial points about the strange inconsistencies surrounding her friend's death, but Daniel argued her suspicions down as mere speculation or the fabricated fantasies of a woman devastated by losing a close friend. Now, an engulfing shame came over him as he understood that he failed her by not listening when she needed his ear above anyone else's. Daniel momentarily looked up to notice Timothy overcome with regret, and he reached out to his friend to get his attention.

"Tim, listen to me. It's not your fault."

"How can you say that? The man is dead, and that country is minus a great leader. It was Ayana's praise of his character that made me reach out to him, and as soon as he heard my proposal, he was in. We'd agreed that his country would finance the entire project if I promised 70 percent of the workforce would be in Southern Sudan to help put his people back to work and give them international trade leverage. He didn't ask for a cut. He didn't ask for some backdoor deal that would make him rich. His only concern was helping his people progress. Very few men like that exist in this world, and one of them is dead because I couldn't keep my mouth shut."

"Wait a minute. Who else did you tell?"

"That bitch from Fox News."

"Huh? Are you telling me you told Kelly Dewitt?"

Timothy remained silent as he nodded his head, refusing to look Daniel in his eyes.

"What? Why? What would possess you to do that?"

"I wasn't thinking, okay? I was so excited about achieving what so many told me was impossible, and since Kelly has the largest audience, I figured she would be the best person to reveal to the world that I beat cancer," Timothy yelled back, jumping forward in his chair and slamming both hands down on the chair's armrest.

"Shhh! Keep your voice down," Daniel warned while looking around to see if any of the passengers were listening in on their conversation. Timothy waved his hand in Daniel's direction and flopped back in his chair.

"I don't even know how I'm going to tell Ayana I got her friend killed."

Oh shit. Hell naw, we not about to even go there right now, Daniel thought.

"I don't think that would be a good idea. Ayana was suspicious of his death, and if you tell her this, she'll be on the first thing smoking to Sudan."

Timothy's forehead immediately crumbled as he turned his head slightly to the left and asked, "So you want me to keep something like this from her?"

"Listen, Tim, I'm trying to keep my wife from doing something crazy. If we tell her about this, she'll put herself in harm's way."

"But she's your wife. Don't you have enough trust between the two of you that . . . wait . . . never mind." Timothy stopped himself once the image of Cloe's fantastic body and ultra blue eyes popped in his head.

My boy ain't shit. I love him, but he ain't shit, Timothy thought while looking Daniel up and down.

"Listen, I know you've just committed sixty million, and God knows I need that money, but at the same time, I can't jeopardize your life or the lives of your family. I'm sitting here thinking, and I'm having reservations about even releasing my findings."

"Don't you dare . . . Don't you fucking dare give in to those animals that killed Alraheem. I made the commitment, and I'm sticking with it. Draw up the paperwork, and you'll have your first investor. My only advice is to keep things quiet until you've secured the actual liquid assets to get this off the ground."

Goes without saying, genius.

"What about Ayana? I'm not going to be able to look her in the eyes, knowing what I know."

"You let me worry about Ayana. I'll handle her."

Yeah, right. As if anyone can handle that woman, Timothy thought, amused.

Leaning forward with a stern look on his face, Timothy pointed his finger at Daniel and replied, "You better fucking tell her, Danny. I know you're gonna need some time, but if you want me to keep my mouth shut . . . you better fucking tell her."

"Tim, I swear, I will tell her. I just have to wait for the right ti—"

"The right time . . . yeah, whatever," Timothy interrupted while nodding his head. "Don't fucking play with me, Danny. There will *never* be a good time. Tell her, or I swear to God—"

Timothy suddenly stopped talking and stared out the window. Noticing he'd reached his stop, he jumped up and quickly exited the train. Daniel stood up and watched his friend run down the stairs of the train to the platform and disappear in the rush-hour crowd. Breathing forcefully, he flopped back down in his chair and placed his head in his hands, trying to deal with a massive headache that was pounding inside his skull.

When will this shit ever end?

Chapter Four

Selfies

Later that evening, Daniel walked through his front door, trying his best to hide the anxiety he felt after he had a few hours to think over everything Timothy told him earlier. He knew that if the president of South Sudan was murdered because of his commitment to invest in Timothy's cure, everyone he cared for was in danger yet again. Three years of preparation wasn't nearly enough to combat what Daniel felt was coming, and he hated to recognize Timothy's mockery of his confidence in his training was spot-on. Dropping his gym bag at the door, Daniel slowly walked into the family room where the heartwarming sounds of Li'l Timothy's laughter filled the room. Timothy suddenly turned toward his father, his eyes sparkling as he jumped to his feet and sprinted in his father's arms.

"Daddy!"

Daniel lifted his son in the air and held him tightly as he closed his eyes in agony. Holding Timothy made things even more challenging as a terrifying thought entered his mind.

What if I'd never gotten involved with Ayana? Would I feel this afraid or helpless? What would my life be like today? Would it be better without her and Li'l Timothy in my life?

Ayana's warm hand running across the back of his neck startled him, and he turned around and tried to kiss her, but she quickly turned away.

"How'd did it go?" she asked coldly.

"I passed," he responded while he searched her eyes, trying to find out what was wrong.

Noticing her cold demeanor, Daniel looked at Ayana and asked, "Baby, what's wrong?"

"I have a lot on my mind," she said, refusing to look at him.

It was at that moment Daniel decided to tell Ayana everything Timothy shared with him earlier. Somehow, he hoped it would keep her from doing something that could put them all in deeper shit than they were already in.

"Timothy stopped by the facility today."

Ayana suddenly burst out into laughter, leaning against Daniel's chest while clinching a handful of material until her tears began to soak through his black athletic shirt. After a minute of laughing hysterically, she sighed while wiping the tears from her eyes.

"I know your instructor didn't let him use the restroom, did he?" she asked, right before she let out a loud cackle and started laughing again until she was almost brought to her knees. Daniel fought with everything he had not to join her in laughter because he knew what he had to tell her next would turn her tears of amusement to pain and rage. Looking up at the ceiling, annoyed, while shaking his head, he slowly put Timothy down and said to him, smiling, "Go play with your toys, Timmy. Daddy and Mommy have to talk about something important, okay?"

Smiling at his father so brightly that it could jump-start a dying sun, Timothy nodded and ran over to his pile of toys sitting in the middle of the family room floor.

Ayana's eyebrows slanted downward as she looked at Daniel's face and noticed he wasn't amused, and she immediately knew something was terribly wrong.

"Danny, what's going on?"

Holding up his index finger, Daniel pulled out his smartphone, and after scrolling over the screen for a few seconds, the house-wide speaker system turned on. Daniel used his finger to push up on his screen, and the volume immediately increased until the entire house was vibrating to the melodic and bass-driven song, "I Will Survive," by Chantay Savage. Satisfied, he held her in his arms and began to whisper everything that Timothy revealed to him on the train. Ayana's first reaction was amazement and pride, but then as Daniel continued to whisper dangerous secrets, her feelings of pride quickly turned to horror. The longer Daniel whispered in her ear, the tighter her embrace became until her hands were grasping at his shirt as if she were hanging on a cliff of pain, overlooking a valley of hopelessness. Daniel could feel her body trembling, and her anger leaking out of every pore of her skin, seeping its engulfing effects into him.

Daniel momentarily glanced over at their son and noticed he was oblivious to their exchange as he held his toy airplane in the air, pretending he was flying across the world. Once Daniel was done, he turned down the music and shouted, "We need to get this system repaired immediately. I can't believe I spent so much money on it, and it malfunctions the way it does."

Nodding in agreement, while wiping the tears from her eyes, Ayana responded, "I'll call the repair guy tomorrow."

"Don't worry about it right now. We have to get ready to go to your friend's funeral. We'll deal with it when we get back."

Hearing Daniel say, "Your friend's funeral," caused a large lump of sorrow to swell in her chest, and Ayana covered her mouth to keep in the wail that was threatening to escape her lips.

"Are you gonna be okay?" Daniel asked while placing both of his hands on her shoulders.

Ayana nodded while wiping more tears from her face. Daniel then walked over to Timothy and began playing with him. Ayana watched the two of them for a few minutes before inhaling deeply and heading into the kitchen. She felt that she had the weight of the world on her shoulders as she tried her best to prepare her husband's dinner without breaking down again. She felt trapped and burdened with mixed feelings of regret, depression, and anger. It's been so long since she felt the connection she and Daniel shared during their fight with Kronte, and even though he came home every night, he wasn't here with her. He was here with Timothy and consumed by his obsession with John Smith. She tried her best to explain away their loss of intimacy, but after over seven months of not being touched by her husband, all kinds of thoughts crept into her mind that made her insecure and petty.

She hated feeling inadequate and unattractive to the man she would die for, and no matter how many times she tried to talk to him about how she felt, he seemed preoccupied with other things besides her. Now, her family could be facing another bout of insanity, and it would definitely push them further away from each other. As she prepared Daniel's plate, she turned toward the family room and watched how involved Daniel was with Timothy, when a frightening thought suddenly entered her mind.

What if he doesn't love me anymore, and he's only with me because of Timothy?

The reality of giving up everything to be a wife and mother—only to find herself alone—sent a chill up her spine, and her hands started to tremble. She quickly placed her husband's plate on the kitchen island and clenched her fists, attempting to stop her hands from shaking. Inhaling deeply, she blew on her hands as if they were freezing, hoping her warm breath would help to stop the uncontrollable vibration in her hands. However, it didn't help, and soon, the waves began to crawl up her arms and creep into her chest. Next, she could feel the nerves in her back spasm and pop as the infecting fear traveled throughout her entire body.

She leaned against the island, trying to prevent herself from falling to the floor. As she tried to open her mouth to call out to Daniel, her eyesight went dark, and she fell. The thud of Ayana's limp body hitting the floor made Daniel jump up and rush into the kitchen.

"Ayana!" he screamed when he saw her body shaking violently while a thick stream of foam flowed out of her mouth.

Four hours later
Highland Park, Illinois
Highland Park Hospital

Daniel sat in the reception area of the emergency room, mentally separated from himself as he frantically tapped the heel of his shoes on the carpeted floor while biting his nails until they began to bleed. Every time the emergency room door opened, he jumped up, expecting the doctor to come out and give him news concerning Ayana, but each time the door opened, it was someone else. A storm of terror raged inside his mind as one word continued to echo in his head: *Poison.*

Somehow, John Smith or someone like him followed him and Timothy and overheard their conversation and decided to murder his wife to send a message.

Suddenly, the hissing sound of the emergency room door opening filled Daniel's ears, and when he leaped to his feet, he noticed it was another patient leaving the hospital with his family. The older man was being wheeled out, flanked by two people who appeared to be his wife and daughter. The patient seemed exhausted yet alert with the relief of his release while looks of worry covered his wife and child's face. Daniel watched them and suddenly felt connected to the mixed feelings the family seemed to display. During his tenure as a doctor, he was all too familiar with the elderlies' disdain of dying in such a mechanical and cold place like a hospital. At the same time, family members felt the fear that their loved one was leaving a place where immediate care could be given if something went wrong.

Running his hand over his forehead and noticing the sweat covering the palm of his hand, Daniel walked over to the water cooler to get himself a cup of water. The cool breeze from the night air blew through the waiting room, and in ran Timothy and Meagan. Both of them appeared terrified as they rushed over to Daniel, standing at the water cooler with a half-filled cup of water in his hand.

"Danny, I got your message! Any news?"

Daniel decided to remain silent and simply shook his head. He feared with all the emotional baggage he was currently carrying, the high-pitched squeal of a teenage girl might come out of his mouth instead of his signature baritone rumble. Timothy noticed the look of defeat and terror on his face and took a few steps back while placing his hand behind the back of his neck. Meagan immediately saw the silent exchange and recognized that the two men knew something that the doctors helping Ayana didn't.

"Wait a minute. What's going on?" Meagan asked while standing between Daniel and Timothy. Daniel's eyes widened as Timothy pointed at him while shaking his head, warning him to keep his mouth shut. Meagan looked at Timothy and gritted her teeth right before she smacked him on his chest.

"My best friend is in there fighting for her life, and you want to keep secrets? What kind of selfish son of a bitch are you?"

Timothy looked down at the spot on his chest where Meagan's open hand just landed with a skin-searing sting. He slowly lifted his eyes and stared into hers, giving her a warning against repeating what she'd just done. Undeterred by his silent warning, Meagan raised her hand to strike Timothy across the face, and he quickly moved closer to her and whispered in her ear, "If you don't want to be next in the emergency room, you shouldn't know the details of what's going on here."

Meagan's eyes widened as her hand slowly fell to her side. With years of experience dealing with certain situations that transpired under the general public's radar, it didn't take her long to understand Timothy's unwillingness to give her the full details. Timothy looked Meagan up and down angrily before he gestured for Daniel to join him outside. Meagan was in a trance as she stood motionless in the middle of the waiting room, like a beautiful blond mannequin. Outside, Timothy and Daniel walked a few paces away from the front door of the hospital.

"Danny, talk to me. What happened?"

"I don't know. I told her everything when I got home, but I made sure I was careful, just in case our house is bugged. Afterward, she went into the kitchen, and the next thing I know, she's on the floor having a seizure."

"My God, what do you think it is?"

"I keep thinking poison, but I hope that's not what it is. Please, God, don't let that be it. Timothy, I swear if they poisoned my wife, I will tear this motherfucker up! I will—"

Timothy placed his hand on his friend's shoulder and nodded his head.

"Let's keep a clear head and hope for the best, Danny. It could be any number of things, so let's just keep a positive outlook."

"They wouldn't even let me back there. Treated me like I was some amateur or something."

"Dude, remember, you gave up your practice once your book blew up," Timothy said with an uncomfortable chuckle. "So technically, they can't allow you back there, but at the same time, I'm sure they know who and what you are. This is one of the best hospitals in the area, so she's in great hands. It's just a good thing you were home when it happened."

Nodding, Daniel responded, "Yeah, you're right. Fuck, dude, I'm a fucking mess," Daniel yelled while smacking himself on the forehead.

"Calm down, bro. Ayana is one of the strongest human beings I know. She'll pull through."

Suddenly, the two men heard the loud clicking sound of heels on concrete, and when they turned around, Meagan was trotting toward them as fast as her four-inch heels would allow.

"They're calling for you, Danny!"

A few seconds later, Daniel was standing in front of Ayana's doctor while he gave them details of what triggered her seizure.

"Doctor Bennett?"

"Yes."

"Pleasure to meet you, sir. Well, we are still running tests to get a complete rundown on what triggered your wife's seizure, but our initial findings show an acute case of malnutrition brought on her seizure. Although she may appear to be healthy, it seems she hasn't been eating properly, probably due to her starving herself, attempting to lose the excess weight she's gained. That, paired with stress, seemed to tip her over the edge. But we were able to stabilize her. She'll have to stay here with us until we get the results of her blood work to make sure there isn't anything else we may be missing."

Daniel looked up at the ceiling, trying to conceal his emotions, and Timothy placed his arm around his friend's shoulder, attempting to console him.

"Can I see her?"

The doctor slowly looked over the three friends and responded, "She's resting, so only you, Doctor Bennett. I can't allow anyone else in there with her until the morning."

Daniel turned to look at Meagan and Timothy, and Meagan quickly nodded and said, "Go ahead, Danny. We'll be here until we can see her."

"Thank you for being here with me."

"Where else would we be?" Timothy responded with a smile. "We got your back, bro. Now, go in there and see your wife."

Daniel quickly embraced his friend and Meagan and slowly followed the doctor through the doors leading into the emergency room. As soon as the door closed behind Daniel, Meagan turned to look Timothy in his eyes with a burning rage that made him take several steps back.

"You are going to tell me *everything*, Timothy, and I don't give a fuck what danger I'm putting myself in. Whether you want to admit it, you both need me to help you navigate whatever bullshit you two have gotten yourselves into. I swear, if either of you instigated this situation by doing something stupid, I will fuck up both of you."

Timothy slightly lowered his head, looked at Meagan, and said, "You're gonna stop threatening me. I'm not quite sure what you're used to at the UN, but here in Chicago, we don't take kindly to threats."

"Fuck your . . ." Meagan paused and then lowered her voice before continuing. "Fuck your city and fuck your feelings. My friend is laid up in there, and there's a possibility that when that blood work comes back, it'll show something *foreign* was introduced into her bloodstream. So, you better come clean, or I'll show you *exactly* how we do things at the UN."

Timothy chuckled while shaking his head and walking away from Meagan, trying to calm down.

This bitc . . . I'm trying to do right. I'm trying to be right. I wanna do right, but she's gonna make a brother revert to the old me if she threatens me one more time.

Turning around, he bumped right into Meagan, who had followed him when he walked away from her. She defiantly stared into his eyes while waiting for him to speak. Sucking his teeth, Timothy grabbed her wrist and pulled her toward the sliding doors leading outside.

Shocked by his aggression, Meagan tried to free herself but soon discovered she could not pull away from him. Once they were outside, he flung Meagan around, so she was standing in front of him. Standing so close to her that she almost became aroused, Timothy looked directly into Meagan's eyes and said, "Don't ever threaten me like that again in your life. First, I'm trying to keep you safe. It's probably too late for me, but not for you. I involved too many people, and this time, I thought I was careful, but apparently, my every move is being watched. I'm praying that whatever happened to Ayana has nothing to do with me, but if it does, trust me when I warn you . . . You don't want to be anywhere near me."

"I don't fucking care, Timothy. We all have been through a lot over the past four years, and if your life is in danger, I want to know why."

Gritting his teeth, he responded, "Okay, have it your fucking way." Timothy leaned forward and began to whisper in her ear aggressively. His words sent waves of mixed emotions through her body, and suddenly, everything started to make sense.

Meagan backed away and started looking around as if she were filled with a feeling of paranoia so engulfing that it seemed the entire world were watching her. Watching her reaction, Timothy nodded his head and said, "Uh-huh. *Now* you understand."

Meagan suddenly stumbled, and Timothy jumped forward, catching her right before she fell backward onto the ground.

"Are you okay?"

Looking up at him with eyes filled with awe and fear, she nodded. "I don't know what to say."

Leaning down while still holding her in his arms, Timothy whispered, "Don't say a damn thing right now. We need to find a place to discuss this freely, but not here."

Looking in Timothy's eyes, Meagan gave him a clear indication she understood and agreed with him. Regaining her balance and standing up on her own, she sighed and wrapped her arms around Timothy's neck. She embraced him with so much warmth, his entire body relaxed, causing him to close his eyes in bliss.

"I love you."

Those three words escaped his lips and caused their entire world to erupt in the fire and brimstones of Pompeii. Meagan immediately released her embrace as her head jerked back. She began searching his eyes, hoping he was playing another one of his childish games, but by the boyish grin on his face, she discovered he was serious.

Oh no, Timothy. You just ruined everything.

"Tim . . . I . . . I—"

"I know what I said is shocking, but I really do love y—"

"Stop, Tim . . . just stop now while there's still time to salvage things. You know I don't have room for love. We discussed this three years ago, and we were both in agreement that this would never be anything but two people satisfying each other's physical cravings."

Breathing forcefully, Timothy responded, "I know that, but you can't expect my feelings to remain the same after three years."

"Uh, yes, I can. What if the shoe were on the other foot?"

"It's not on the other foot. It's on mines. I'm not asking you to say you love me back or even love me today. I'm just asking you to consider opening yourself up to love me. Is that too much to ask after three years?"

Meagan shuffled her feet as she looked down at her black four-inch heels, shaking her head. A long, excruciating silence followed that sent Timothy's emotions in a frenzy, but he forced himself to remain calm and seem as if he were unbothered by her silence. Sniffing and clearing her throat, Meagan lifted her head and said, "Yes, Timothy, that's far too much to ask of me right now. I don't ever want to hurt you or make you feel like you're not relationship material, but my life just doesn't have room for what you're asking of me. I'm sorry, Timothy, but we can't see each other intimately any longer. I hope we can still remain friends, but if not, I completely understand."

She then planted a soft kiss on his cheek and walked back into the hospital, leaving Timothy outside in complete shock. It's been over fifteen years since he felt the searing burn of rejection, but the wound it reopened felt as if it were only yesterday. Folding his full lips into his mouth, Timothy cleared his throat and slowly walked back into the hospital. Once inside, he looked over at Meagan, sitting on the far side of the waiting room, and he nodded his head in recognition. She pretended she didn't see him looking at her and continued to look at the wall-mounted television across from her seat. Clearing his throat and adjusting his black, designer, wool peacoat, Timothy walked to the other side of the room, took a seat facing the large windows, and closed his eyes, pretending to fall asleep.

Meagan slightly turned her head and peeked over at Timothy. He seemed calm and unbothered by her rejection. What she couldn't see was the war of emotions raging inside of him. His body temperature had increased until he was sweating through his clothing under his coat. The chaos of his thoughts made him angry one second and then heartbroken the next. A few times, he considered leaving, but he knew Ayana and Daniel needed him here.

I just pray things don't get too weird and uncomfortable between us . . . Who am I fooling? This shit is gonna get weird as fuck, Meagan thought, as she continued to watch Timothy sleep.

Five hours later, the three friends stood inside Ayana's hospital room, watching her eat a cup of fruit. Ayana seemed oblivious to their stares of worry as she devoured the fruit cup, making it appear as if she hadn't eaten in weeks. Once she finished eating that, she reached for a slice of wheat toast, and Daniel cleared his throat loudly, startling her while gaining her attention.

"Baby, how do you feel?"

Swallowing the remaining fruit in her mouth, Ayana smiled and responded, "I'm feeling much better. Just hungry as hell. Where's Li'l Timmy?"

"He's at my parents. We are all relieved you are feeling better, but we are concerned because the results came back, and the doctors believe you've been starving yourself to lose weight."

Ayana rolled her eyes and reached for the carton of orange juice sitting on her food tray. She then closed her eyes and drank down the juice, allowing its cold and refreshing citrus flavor to wash down the dry feeling she felt in her throat. Once she was done, she calmly reached for the second carton of orange juice on her tray and began drinking it while keeping everyone else in suspense.

Angered by her uncaring attitude, Daniel thundered, "I know you heard what I said, Ayana. You don't have to be embarrassed. We're amongst family, so tell me why you have been starving yourself."

She looked in Daniel's eyes with disdain so livid that it caused a whistle of shock to escape Timothy's lips. Ayana then slowly lowered the carton of juice from her mouth and responded. "I figured if I were on my deathbed, you would set aside a few hours for me instead of spending all your time at the training facility with that blue-eyed heifer, Cloe."

Timothy's tired and half-closed eyelids immediately popped wide open. He then cleared his throat and turned around while whispering, "Damn."

At the same time, unable to hide her surprise, Meagan yelled out, "Oh shit." Embarrassed, she immediately apologized and covered her mouth when Daniel and Ayana turned and looked at her.

"Ayana, maybe we should talk about this later."

"Oh no, you wanted to discuss my medical situation while everyone's here, so let's let it all hang out. We're amongst family, right?"

Daniel started twisting his neck around, trying to loosen the stress that seemed to tighten the muscles around his shoulders. Running his hand down his mouth to his chin, he inhaled and said, "Fine, if that's what you want."

"Wait. Stop it, you two," Meagan protested. "This is not the time for the two of you to come unhinged. We should be happy you are doing better, and although the results are alarming, they could've been worse, given the situation."

"Meagan's right. We shouldn't be arguing," Daniel agreed.

"I don't give a damn about what Meagan is saying, and fuck what you're talking about. I want to know who Cloe is to you. I'm not going to let this go, especially after receiving an anonymous email yesterday afternoon, full of pictures of you and her at the training facility . . . selfies and shit. You two seemed really into each other, all hugged up and having a fantastic time in each other's arms. The way you smiled at her in those pictures is the way you *used* to smile at me. Now, it's glowing for another woman. So, who is she to you, and I'm going to cut through the red tape and ask . . . Are you fucking her?"

After hearing Ayana's rant, Timothy suddenly flopped down in the chair behind Daniel and buried his head in his hands. Meagan's eyebrows lifted while leaning over to look Daniel in his eyes, and her mouth flung open as she gasped, "Danny!"

Wiping his forehead, Daniel turned away from Meagan and moved to the other side of Ayana's bed toward the window. Looking outside at the concrete roof and massive air vents protruding out of the roof of the buildings outside the window, he shook his head and chuckled.

"To answer your question . . . no. I'm not having an affair with Cloe—or any other woman for that matter."

"Oh, you're having an affair, Doctor Bennett," Ayana snapped. "You just may not have sealed the deal by inserting your dick into her. But, oh, make no mistake, mister, you're having an affair."

"That doesn't make any sense. Are you saying a married man can't have friends of the opposite sex without it being an affair?"

"Yes!" Everyone in the room responded to his question.

"Your wife is all the friends with a vagina you'll ever need," added Meagan. "I can see if this was an old high school or college buddy, but I'm assuming this Cloe ho isn't going to be showing up at the reunion."

"No. He's only known her for a little over three months," Ayana yelled, "and he's already taking selfies and shit with her!"

Those selfies really got her in her feelings, Timothy thought, amused, while attempting to hide a smirk.

"Are you finding this funny, Timothy?" Ayana asked, staring at him with her eyes nearly closed and her nostrils flaring.

Meagan spun around just in time to catch Timothy's grin—right before he adopted a more serious facial expression.

"You knew about Cloe?" Meagan asked Timothy angrily.

Shaking his head so violently his lips began to flap, he responded, "Don't put me in the middle of this. I was banned from the facility *years* ago, remember?"

"Don't remind me," Meagan responded, rolling her eyes and shaking her head.

And he wants a serious relationship? Yeah, like I'm prescribing to that brand of stupid.

"Whatever, Timothy. You two are always keeping each other's secrets," Ayana yelled.

"Exactly," Meagan agreed.

Jumping to his feet, Timothy pointed at Ayana and Meagan and said, "That's rich, coming from the two of you, isn't it? You two are the queens of secrets. You could have your own *Indiana Jones* adventure series with all the hidden shit you two hold in. So, let's not go there. And like I told you before, keep *me* out of this. I'm not your husband, neither is Meagan, and I think it's fucked up that you are talking about this right now in front of us. We may be family, but we aren't married to either of you. Daniel may be stupid . . . sorry, bro . . . but the last thing he will ever be is unfaithful to you."

Ayana sucked her teeth and waved Timothy off. She then turned toward Daniel, who remained silent as he looked out the window.

"Are you going to say anything, Daniel?" she asked.

Shaking his head, Daniel folded his arms and just continued to look out the window.

"So, you're ignoring me? Well, I guess you've done it for so long, it's become second nature to you. I bet if I were that bitch asking you a question, you would jump out of your skin to answer her."

Daniel spun around and was about to respond, but he closed his eyes and stopped himself. Waving his index finger at Ayana, Daniel let out an aggravated chuckle and turned back around to the window.

"It's okay. The doctor said I could go home today, which gives me enough time to get Li'l Timothy and get ready to travel."

Daniel's eyes nearly popped out of his head as he turned around with a look of anger so primal, it momentarily startled everyone in the room.

"You don't want to play with me like that, Ayana," he said, in a whispered growl that sent chills through her.

Wanting to show him his aggressive behavior didn't intimidate her, Ayana responded, "You can't stop me, even if you tried. I will take my son with me to bury my friend. You can stay here and work things out with Cloe since you're not willing to work them out with your wife."

"Your friend won't be the only burial if you—"

"Whoa. Okay, that's enough. We're leaving now," Timothy interrupted while waving his hands in the air. "Danny, let's go. I'm sure Meagan can get Ayana home safely. Ayana, it's great that you're doing better. Meagan, it's been real."

Timothy then snatched Daniel by his arm and pushed him out of the room. Once the door closed behind them, Meagan slowly moved to the side of the bed and sat down next to Ayana. Ayana looked down at her hands without saying a word. She was shocked and terrified that the man she'd given everything to—the man she would die for—would threaten her.

She suddenly felt the familiar sickening lump in her stomach that Kronte gave her many years ago every time he raped, beat, and threatened her. She could feel it build up in her chest, affecting her heartbeat and increasing her blood flow. Her hands grew cold, and the muscles along her back pulled and throbbed. It traveled up her torso, moving through her lungs, making them swell and contract violently. It climbed up her throat and forcefully sprang out of her mouth like a trumpet, announcing the agony of a heartbroken and devastated woman. Her eyes flooded like the levees of New Orleans, pouring down her face and drenching her dark coffee cheeks.

Meagan's heart ached for her friend, watching her cry hysterically. She felt useless because she knew relationships weren't her strong point. She'd never found a reason to give of herself to anyone to the point that their actions brought her to tears. She couldn't comprehend the heartbreak from a man's actions or the hopelessness of a failing relationship that you wanted to succeed. So, she did the only thing she could. She wrapped her arms around Ayana and allowed her to release the emotions that were killing her inside.

***

A few minutes later, Timothy and Daniel walked into the parking lot of the hospital. Timothy's mind was thrown into a constant loop, replaying everything that Ayana said in the room, and he tried to keep his mouth shut, but eventually, his curiosity got the best of him.

"Danny, keep it real with me, bro. Did you fuck Cloe?"

Daniel stopped walking and paused for a second as he stared blankly into the distance. *I can't believe he has the nerve to ask me that.*

Turning with his head tilted and his mouth twisted to the side of his face, he responded, "Tim, you already know I didn't fuck that girl. Why would you even think I did?"

"Uh, pictures, selfies, and other shit. I've never known you to roll like that when you're in a serious relationship. In all my years of knowing you, I've never seen or heard that."

"Maybe because I keep my dirt to myself," Daniel responded sarcastically.

"Dude, you're not helping my anxiety. You have an amazing woman. Given, she's not perfect, but she loves you, and you're acting like this shit don't matter."

"I'm sorry, but my mind isn't on this emotional shit."

"Dude, you're about to lose your family, and this ain't on your mind?"

"No. Because I know where my dick's been, and it hasn't been in Cloe. Granted, she's a beautiful woman; yes, she's attracted to me; and, yes, I may have taken some pictures that I shouldn't have. I agree it's stupid, but what's concerning me above all the petty shit is that *all* the pictures she's talking about, all the selfies that have everyone all up in their feelings? Those were all taken on my phone and deleted before I got home."

"Huh? That's impossible. Maybe you forgot to remove some of the pictures," Timothy responded.

"Highly doubtful because I always erase my memory on my phone each day. It's become second nature to me. Clearing out your digital footprint each day was one of the first lessons we learned under Ruiz."

"Then maybe Cloe didn't delete her photos and sent them to Ayana. Did you consider that?"

"Nope."

"Huh? What da fuck you mean, nope?" *This mother-fucker here is sprung on that Cloe bitch, and he hasn't even smelled the pussy.*

"Daniel, are you seriously telling me you don't suspect Cloe of being the one who sent those photos?"

"That's *exactly* what I'm telling you. What is the number one rule I taught you about women?"

"Man, Danny, I don't have time for a Playa 101 refresher."

"What was the number one rule, Tim?"

"Dude—"

"What was it?"

"Never let a bitch take your picture with her phone if you got a woman already," Timothy responded, slowly reciting each word while rolling his eyes and rocking his head from side to side.

"There you go, young Padawan learner. The Force is still strong with you," Daniel teased. "I never let her take a picture of us together with her phone. They were all taken on my phone. She asked me repeatedly to send her copies of our pics together, and I never did. So now that we got that out of the way . . . Do you understand why I have more important things to worry about than Ayana's temper tantrum?"

Timothy looked at Daniel and shook his head. Grunting loudly while throwing up his hands, Daniel responded,

"Someone else sent those photos. Someone who has the power to access the servers that store all communications over cellular networks."

Suddenly, Timothy's eyes widened, and his mouth slowly opened as he appeared to be having an epiphany. Then as suddenly as his "light in the dark" expression appeared, it vanished. In its place came a look of disbelief as his eyelids lowered halfway down over his eyes.

"I knew training at that facility was going to drive you crazy. Dude, I promise you your extramarital activities with big booty Cloe are no concern of the type of people you're referring to. Just admit you got caught slipping and make it right with your wife."

"I thought you of all people would understand what's going on."

"Oh, I understand, and that's why I'm not buying your bullshit. I'm not judging you, bro . . . well, maybe a little. Cloe is a bad muthafucka, no doubt, but compared to Ayana, Cloe is a downgrade in every department. Make this shit right, Danny. A lot of people risked their lives and careers to see you two together, and I'll be damned if I let you throw it away on a bitch that ain't even worthy."

"None of you will ever understand until the storm is at your doorstep."

"Whatever, Noah. Fix it. You hear me? Fix this shit!" Timothy yelled as he snatched open his car door.

Daniel didn't move as he watched Timothy climb into his 2016 Mercedes S 63 and drive off. As he climbed into his car, an alarming thought popped into Daniel's mind, and he decided he'd better stop by Ruiz's training facility before going to pick up his son.

Chapter Five

Starting New Fires with Old Flames

Later that morning, Timothy sat in his office, staring at the wall like a man in a trance. The white walls and abstract paintings seemed to morph into a whirlpool of blacks and whites that urged him to fall deeper down the rabbit hole of madness. He felt his life had come to a standstill, although he had one of the most important vaccines in human history. But without the proper funding and security, he might as well have discovered an obscure stone from one of the sandy beaches along Lake Michigan.

As he started to doze off, his secretary's voice blasted through the intercom.

"Doctor Avers, you have a visitor."

Surprised out of his near nap, Timothy sat up and asked, "Who is it?"

"It's Mr. Maximillian Karlov."

"What? *The* Maximillian Karlov?"

"Yes, Doctor Avers."

Timothy sat up in a daze as he tried to comprehend why one of the wealthiest men in the world would be at his office. Understanding a man like Maximillian Karlov has very little patience, he instructed his secretary to show him into his office, and he got up from his desk to greet him at the door. When the door opened, nothing could prepare him for whom stood in his office doorway, smiling with a welcoming hand extended. Timothy's mouth hung open as the world around him seemed to move in slow motion. His eyes delighted over every inch of her, inhaling her perfume, a combination of scents that jump-started a memory from the past that flooded his entire body with feelings of yearning, pain, lust, and rejection. Her dark, Godiva chocolate-covered skin was flawless, and the business suit she wore made love to every curve on her fantastic body. Looking her over transported Timothy to a time when he vacationed between her thighs, embarking on some of the best sexual experiences of his life.

Goddamn, she still looks amazing.

Slowly reaching out to shake her hand, Timothy swallowed the saliva threatening to drool out of his mouth, and said, "Simone Rose? What a surprise to see you here. I had no idea you worked for Mr. Karlov."

As soon as he noticed Timothy's reaction to his wife, he quickly stepped in front of her while extending his massive hand.

"That's Simone *Karlov,* now," the six foot three, 230-pound Russian interjected in a thick Russian accent. Timothy almost choked on his own saliva as he looked at Simone and then at the 62-year-old billionaire, who was now smiling proudly at Timothy's look of amazement.

"I'm sorry. I had no idea, Mr. Karlov."

"Oh, that's fine," Mr. Karlov responded while firmly shaking Timothy's hand. "I understand you and my wife were classmates at Northwestern."

"Classmates?" Timothy responded while giving Simone a suspicious look.

"Yes . . . classmates," Mr. Karlov replied, smiling brightly while holding Timothy's hand and increasing the pressure of his grip.

Oh, this asshole is pissing on the hydrant.

"Oh yes. Classmates," Timothy responded, nodding his head while slowly repeating "classmates."

Mr. Karlov's piercing gray eyes sent Timothy a clear warning not to take a stroll down memory lane with his young, Black, and beautiful trophy wife. Timothy slowly nodded, giving Maximillian his silent agreement, and the two men relaxed as Timothy showed Mr. Karlov and Simone into his office.

"Have a seat, please," Timothy said as he closed the door behind them. Sitting behind his desk, Timothy looked at his visitors and asked, "How can I help you?"

"The question isn't how can you help us, but how can *we* help *you*."

"I'm sorry, I don't follow."

"Cut the shit, Doctor. We know what you have, and I would like to invest in your vaccine," Maximillian snapped.

"H-h-how do you know about that?" Timothy stuttered.

"Doctor Avers, I am worth over forty billion dollars, and for me to maintain and increase my net worth, I have to be a man that stays current on the next big thing. What you have is going to change the world and make an ungodly amount of money in the process, and I want in. I understand your initial investor is no longer in the game, so I am here to fill his space with my money and influence."

"Influence?"

"Doctor Avers, wealth brings privilege, and I have the privilege to have the direct ear of the FDA. I can get you the green light for human trials and then final approval within a year. Now, can anyone else deliver that kind of influence, as well as put six hundred million dollars into your bank account?"

"My max budget estimates are four hundred and fifty million, Mr. Karlov."

"Well, that should give you what I like to call a 'fucked-up contingency fund,' just in case things don't go as smoothly as you anticipate."

"Mr. Karlov, forgive me for my lack of faith in your 'privilege' pitch. Your wealth comes from transportation, fuel, and black-market arms sales, am I correct?"

Mr. Karlov's head jerked backward as he cleared his throat and looked over at Simone. Watching his shocked and uncomfortable reaction, Timothy grinned and responded, "Yeah, I know things too. But my concern isn't your access to weapons, because frankly, it may come in handy one day. No, my concerns are the fact you don't have any investments in the pharmaceutical industry. So how can you influence the FDA?"

"The fact I don't have investments in the pharmaceutical industry is the sole reason why your vaccine is so valuable to me. I will only gain from this, unlike those who do have investments in the pharmaceutical industry. You're going against immensely powerful people, and without me, your vaccine will never get through the final FDA approval process. The FDA is a business, and don't let the word 'federal' in its name fool you into believing otherwise. What you are attempting to do will shift the entire landscape of modern medicine forever. Drugs, treatments, facilities, doctors, education, etcetera, will become obsolete overnight. We are talking about billions of dollars in profits lost once your vaccine is approved. Do you think those whose bottom line will be adversely affected by your vaccine will allow your cure to be approved if you go this alone? You're questioning my influence, but tell me, Doctor, do you even *know* the janitor at FDA headquarters?"

Timothy looked away and remained silent. An antagonizing smile grew on Simone's face as she watched the usually talkative and sarcastic doctor silenced by her husband.

"So sensitive, but sure, Doctor. We are clear."

Timothy looked over at Daniel, who was looking down at the floor with his body slumped and defeated. Timothy shook his head at his friend, feeling angry and helpless, but he knew he had to cater to Ayana's petty behavior if he wanted to try to save their lives.

"Fine, Ayana. I'll speak with you alone, but I want you to know what you are doing to your husband is fucked up, and it will come back to bite you in the ass. Let's go."

Frowning while rolling her eyes, Ayana followed him into her bedroom so the two of them could talk. Daniel watched them walk into Ayana's bedroom and sighed forcefully.

She didn't even look at me. It's like I don't exist to her any longer, he thought as he retreated to the balcony alone.

Once inside Ayana's room, she closed the door behind them, flopped down on her bed, and gestured for Timothy to start talking. Her cold demeanor almost made him yell, "Fuck it and fuck you," and storm out of her room, but he cared about her, and the last thing he wanted was for his godson to grow up without a mother. Nevertheless, he wasn't going to allow her to play with him as she played with Daniel, so he decided to set the tone early.

"Listen, I really don't have time to play the attitude game with you, Ayana, so can you, at least, *pretend* you care about me almost getting shot to tell you this."

Ayana slowly looked up at Timothy with eyes filled with regret. His statement of almost getting shot made her realize that she'd shut out everyone, even those that deserved her gratitude and respect. So, she nodded and gave him her full attention. Noticing her change of attitude, Timothy pulled a chair closer to the foot of the bed and sat down directly in front of her. Looking Ayana in her eyes, he said, "You have to drop out of this election—immediately."

Ayana's blood immediately started to boil, and she moved farther back on her bed, increasing the distance between them. Timothy's eyes widened when he noticed her reaction, and he looked at her as if she'd just lost her mind.

"Did Daniel put you up to this?"

"What . . . wait . . . huh? Put me up to what?"

"Put you up to convince me to drop out of the election—*that's* what."

"No. Hell no. The last time I spoke to Danny, he warned me not to come over here. My reasons for not wanting you to run with Patrick is because that man has a plan, which may not be in your country's best interest."

Timothy's statement piqued Ayana's curiosity, so she moved closer to him so that she wouldn't miss anything he might tell her.

"How do you know this?"

"I just met with him less about an hour ago."

"With Patrick Djeng? The president?"

"Yes, we were supposed to discuss how we would move forward with opening a production site for my vaccine, and he turned me down flat, telling me that he didn't want to offend the 'wrong' people by helping me bankrupt the entire pharmaceutical industry."

Ayana remained silent for a few seconds before responding. "Selfish and self-centered."

"Exactly, and I don't think you want to run with a ma—"

"I wasn't talking about Patrick. I was referring to you."

"Huh? Me?"

"Yeah, you, Timothy. Just because Patrick turned you down, you've decided he couldn't be trusted. When you consider his statement of not wanting to offend the wrong people, which is an excellent point, I'm even prouder to run alongside the man. The only individuals in this entire scenario that can't be trusted are you and my 'husband.'"

"Me? Why me? I am *not* your husband."

"No, but you're his best friend, and you two share everything. Including information about side pieces."

"Oh no. Don't you dare put me between you and Danny."

"So, are you gonna sit there and tell me you didn't know about Cloe until the night you came to our house to patch up John?"

Timothy looked down at the floor while shuffling his feet. Ayana leaned down so that she could look Timothy in his eyes, and as soon as he noticed what she was doing, he turned away.

"Exactly. You knew, and you didn't come to my front door to warn me about that scandalous bitch and my husband, but you have the nerve now to tell me about Patrick? Do you *really* expect me to take your word on this?"

"Yes, I do because this is serious. This isn't some misunderstanding between you and Danny. This is about your life and the lives of millions of your people. But I can see by your attitude that you ain't trying to hear a word I'm saying. So instead of sitting here wasting another second of my time, I'ma just leave."

Timothy then got up and walked to the door. Right before he opened it to leave, he turned and looked at Ayana with eyes filled with a deep and personal anger she'd never before felt from him. His enraged gaze caused goose bumps to blanket her entire body.

"I will tell you this once, Ayana. If anything happens to Li'l Timmy or Danny because of you and your allegiance to Patrick . . ."

And without verbally finishing his sentence, yet making it entirely clear what he was saying, he flung open the door and stormed out.

That's the second time someone I thought cared for me has threatened me.

"Call me a cab, so I can leave this godforsaken place," Timothy said to Daniel as he stood in the doorway leading out to the balcony. Daniel turned around and looked at his friend with a tortured revelation that startled Timothy. Ayana was lost to them and was now finding trust in people that had more to gain by betraying her than being loyal to her. Seeing his friend's expression broke Timothy's heart, but he knew he couldn't stay any longer. He had a world of things to do, and staying here to help his friend would only undermine his efforts. It was either Daniel or the world, and this time, Timothy had to choose the latter. It was the first time in their lives as friends that Timothy had to choose someone or something else over their friendship. And it was the hardest choice he's ever had to make.

Daniel nodded and slowly walked past Timothy to make the phone call. As he neared his friend, Daniel refused to look Timothy in the eyes. The shame and heartbreak were too much, and the last thing he wanted to do was lose his shit in front of his friend.

Timothy continued to look forward as if the view from the balcony was much more important than the painful walk of shame his best friend was taking inside the villa. He closed his eyes tightly, attempting to rid the memory of the look on his friend's face and then decided to step out on the balcony to get some much-needed fresh air.

I'm sorry, brother. But you're on your own this time.

Chapter Twelve

Deadly Debate

Two weeks later
Bor, South Sudan

As soon as John Garang Memorial University's auditorium started to fill up, Ayana quickly discovered the four-hour, heavily guarded ride to Mading-Bor, located in the eastern state of Jonglei, was the least uncomfortable part of her day. The eyes of those in the audience were filled with a potent cocktail of malice, fear, and hatred that made the auditorium feel as though it were equipped with top-of-the-line central air-conditioning. Patrick sat on her left side, sweat pouring from every pore on his face, causing his ultra dark skin to shine in the afternoon sunlight, streaming through the open windows lining the walls of the large meeting room. He seemed unbothered by the tension building in the room as people entered. The room was quickly filling beyond capacity, and the combination of the glaring sunlight and body heat made the atmosphere steam like a sauna.

Trying her best to appear to be enjoying the experience, Ayana began to notice the people's tattered attire and worn-out shoes and sandals.

Farmers . . . This place is filled with poor farmers. How are we gonna get these people to understand the big picture? They need help now, and they don't want to wait for years to get it. This is far worse than I thought.

Looking to her right, John Smith stood next to the end of the table with his hands interlocked in front of his groin while he attentively surveyed the growing crowd. Not a bead of sweat poured from his light, sand-colored skin, unaffected by the suffocating heat. Watching him carefully, Ayana began to wonder what kind of training his body had to endure to withstand this level of exterior punishment and show no signs that it was affecting him. Considering her own past and how brutal her training was, she couldn't imagine the horrors John had to put his body through to become the top assassin in the world.

Across the stage was another large wooden table, with their opponent, Thomas Bossa, seated alone with an aura of confidence that seemed to infect everyone in the room, including Ayana. He seemed too sure of himself as if he already knew the outcome of this debate in the largest and most impoverished state in South Sudan. Thomas hadn't named a running mate, and according to his statements in the media, *"He could defeat Patrick and his Americanized UN puppet single-handedly."* The remainder of his statement made Ayana's teeth grit as she tried to calm the growing anger inside her.

Closing her eyes, Ayana tried to calm her nerves until the sudden echo of the auditorium's doors closing filled the room, making her jump in her chair. The loud chatter inside the auditorium subsided as the debate moderator, Daniel Panyang, son of Jonglei's governor, began to speak.

"Today, we will hear from the candidates in the upcoming elections and listen to what they plan to do to make things better for the people of Jonglei. Our state has suffered for decades from war and famine, and under a new regime, we demand our concerns be made relevant. So, for either candidate to receive our votes, we decided to invite them here to discuss their plans for the future of our nation and Jonglei. We will start with the current president, Patrick Djeng. Gentlemen, please make your way to the podiums."

Ayana immediately began clapping ferociously. The sharp sound of her hands colliding traveled to every corner of the auditorium, and she was so engulfed in her excitement, she didn't notice that she was the only one clapping. Every pair of eyes was fixed on the silly-looking beauty as she continued to clap wildly. The look of disgust on their faces gave Patrick the feeling they all believed she was the source of the Ebola virus or some other incurable disease.

Patrick quickly reached over and held her wrist tightly while drawing her attention to the crowd's reaction—or lack thereof. Ayana immediately stopped clapping and placed her hands on top of the dark wooden table. Patrick slowly stood to his feet, adjusted his tie, and strolled over to the podium to the soundtrack of dead silence. Not even the buzzing wings of the giant African flies or the heels of his expensive Italian shoes made a sound as he made his way to the podium.

Thomas watched the duo while shaking his head and then walked over to the other podium that stood a few feet away from Patrick. Once behind the podium, Thomas Bossa ran his hand under his bearded chin while maintaining a stern look on his face. Looking over the crowd, he stared into their eyes like a man possessed with purpose. Thomas was a large, intimidating man, who used his size and demeanor to his advantage every time the opportunity presented itself, and today, the opportunity was ripe for the taking.

Looking at both candidates and making sure they were ready, the moderator began the debate.

"First question, President Djeng, how will you solve the many issues of the country's lack of basic infrastructures like clean water and energy?"

"Well, we have plans to increase our gross national income by using our number one resource, crude oil, as a trade commodity. With the projected revenue from selling the resource on the world markets, South Sudan will be able to use that income to bring clean water and energy to every corner of the country."

The moderator nodded his head and then turned to Thomas and said, "Same question, Mr. Bossa."

"Unlike the clueless man next to me, I plan to use our crude oil deposits to finance our infrastructure, but at a much-faster pace. You see, the acting president's plan to corner the world market by only allowing Southern Sudanese people to drill and process the oil and enabling us to set our own prices will take several years, if not longer, to complete. During that time, the people of South Sudan will continue to suffer from hunger, unemployment, and war. I plan to get our oil out of the ground and into the tanks of cars worldwide in less than a year by allowing foreign companies to come in here and harvest the oil. This will create not only high-paying jobs but also generate international interest in our country. Our people need this now, *not* years down the line.

"We are hungry and poor, yet we literally are floating on black gold, but if the president has his way, the oil will stay in the ground until we can do it ourselves. The people are starving, and we can't eat the oil, so let's get it out of the ground now and fill hungry bellies and put our people to work."

Thomas pumped his fist in the air as he closed out his statement, expecting the people to join him, but they were unmoved by his passionate speech. He swallowed hard as he noticed the drowning silence and slowly lowered his arm to his side. Smiling at the embarrassment of his opponent, Patrick nodded his head and responded, "We are a young nation, and, yes, we are hungry and poor, but if we want to compete in this world, we have to be independent. We must educate ourselves on how to take advantage of what we have. Bringing in foreign interest will only make foreigners rich and increase their country's national gross income, not South Sudan's. I believe, unlike my opponent, that we are, in fact, more than capable. I believe through patience and education, we can be better than any foreign power that would come in here and exploit our resources and our people."

"You liar!" The booming sound of those two words being yelled from the crowd traveled to every ear in the auditorium. Startled, Patrick started to look through the crowd to find his accuser, but he didn't have to look long because his accuser pushed his way through the crowd until he was standing front and center. The man's eyes were crimson with rage, and his sweat-covered face was crumbled and scarred from the many years of living in such a hostile territory of the country.

The moderator quickly tried to take control of the situation, but the angry farmer refused to acknowledge Daniel Panyang as he continued to yell, "You are all liars! You insult us by coming here and telling things that we all know aren't true. None of you are concerned about the people. You are only concerned about lining your pockets."

"Hold on, that's not true. I'm trying to keep our most valuable natural resource under South Sudanese control," Patrick responded.

The man's eyes slowly began to shrink into small slits as he listened to Patrick explain his position.

"You think because we've never had your fancy education, or because you wear fancy suits and shoes that we don't know what you're planning to do?"

"We are planning to take this country into the future," Thomas added, the rumbling tone of his voice seemingly vibrating the walls of the building.

"No—you are planning to rape us and then leave us all to die."

"What is your name?" Patrick asked in a noncombative tone, attempting to suppress any escalations.

"My name is Asim Mahmorah."

The sound of the angry man's name caused everyone to hold their breath at the realization a man thought to be dead was alive, well, and very furious. Asim was a legend and hero to the people of Jonglei. He was an ultraorthodox man of Christian faith and a freedom fighter during the war with Northern Sudan. If there was any man with the voice to ignite the people of Jonglei, Asim Mahmorah was that man.

Patrick immediately felt the tiny hairs on his arms rise, and the sweat on the back of his neck turn frigid. Ayana was in a daze as she slowly stood to her feet to get a closer look at the man she'd admired and feared her entire life. Asim's presence equally moved Thomas, and he took two steps back from the podium while looking toward his security detail, making sure they were on as high of an alert as he was.

"Mr. Mahmorah, you honor us with your presence." The words flowed out of Ayana's mouth with a poetic reverence that demanded Asim's attention. The very sight of Ayana seemed to relax Asim immediately, and he sighed peacefully while opening his eyes completely to take in all of her splendor.

"Mrs. Bennett, you and your family are only pawns in their game. You are just a beautiful distraction, paraded around the country like an expensive whore. Whatever power these men led you to believe you have is just an illusion. Those with real power are standing at the podium if you haven't noticed, and those without are not. Accept the obvious and understand that the sound of your voice is not welcomed here."

The calm demeanor in which Asim insulted Ayana was so flawlessly executed that it took her about thirty seconds to comprehend exactly what he was saying to her. Her smile slowly evaporated from her face as his words cut deep. Her nostrils began to flare, and her breathing became labored and aggressive. As angry as she was, Ayana knew that responding in kind to a man like Asim would be a mistake—a deadly one. So, she flashed him a sarcastic smile and sat back down in her seat without saying another word.

Satisfied that his point was received, Asim turned his attention to the two men vying for the presidency and said, "The people of South Sudan and Jonglei will no longer sit idle and allow puppets to rape and pillage our home. The nonsense stops *now*."

Suddenly, a portion of the crowd separated, revealing a large group of men armed with machetes and large wooden planks of wood covered in barbed wire. Before the armed guards posted at the door could react, Asim's men had overrun and viciously attacked them. The rest of the crowd retreated to the floor, lying flat on the ground, trying to avoid the rapid gunfire that erupted from the security personnel's weapons that accompanied the two candidates. As the earsplitting sound of gunfire and screams of terror erupted throughout the auditorium, Asim looked toward Ayana, who was crouched under the table.

He quickly began to make his way over toward her with a group of seven men surrounding him like a protective circle. Asim moved like a man twenty years younger as he effortlessly leaped atop the six-foot-high stage and quickly moved closer to Ayana's hiding place. John, noticing Asim's intentions, quickly moved to intercept them before they got too close to her. Seeing John moving closer to him, Asim immediately ordered his men to take John down while he dealt with Ayana.

Finally, lunch, John thought, right before he began to engage Asim's men. Two of the men attacked first, swinging for the assassin's head. John quickly ducked under their dual attacks, pulled out his sidearm and fired two shots into their chests and one shot under both their chins, sending them flying backward and off the stage. Another attacker swung his machete toward John's left leg, and John quickly lifted his leg, leaned forward, placed the muzzle of his gun on the attacker's temple, and pulled the trigger. Another attacker, seeing an opening, attacked from behind, but John ducked under and to the right. Standing next to the attacker, John swung his left arm backward, striking the man in his throat with the butt of his gun, crushing his throat. John then fired another shot in the choking attacker's head, causing the other side of his head to explode in blood, bone, and brain matter.

The other three attackers paused for a second as they watched their numbers go from seven to three in seconds. Their hesitation was more time than John needed to bring the fight to them. Before they could respond, John appeared directly in front of them, bombarding them with bullets and deadly strikes. As the remaining three men's bodies fell lifelessly to the floor below the stage, John turned his gun toward Ayana's direction to put a bullet in the back of Asim's head. However, when he looked, he noticed Ayana twisting Asim's body around and then slamming his head onto the table. She then came down on the back of his neck with her forearm, rendering him unconscious and probably giving him a concussion in the process.

Watching her expertly take down a seasoned soldier as if he were a Boy Scout caused John's entire body to tingle as a satisfied smile shined on his face. Ayana looked up and noticed his proud stare, and without thinking, she returned the favor. She then rushed to his side, and the two of them jumped down from the stage and began to fight their way toward the exit. Looking ahead of her through the violence and chaos, Ayana noticed Patrick and Thomas were both moving through the crowd, their depleted security teams joining forces to get them out of the auditorium alive.

"Patrick," Ayana called out to her friend, and he quickly turned around. Patrick then tapped the shoulder of the closest soldier to him and said, "We need to get Ayana and her man out of here too."

"Sir, I'm sorry, but we don't have time for that. You are the president, and we must get *you* out of here. Ayana Bennett is not a priority." Without further explanation, the soldier continued to fight and shoot his way out of the auditorium. Patrick momentarily looked back again as a host of insurgents surrounded her and John. They were outnumbered, and although both skilled fighters, Patrick knew neither of them would make it out of the auditorium alive without their help. The thought made him close his eyes, shaking his head in remorse, as his men managed to kick open the doors of the hall and escort the two candidates outside to safety.

Two hours later
Juba, South Sudan

"Where the fuck is my wife?" Daniel screamed into the phone. He'd been on the telephone for over an hour once the local news reported the attack on the debate in Bor. Daniel continued to pace back and forth in the living area of the villa with Li'l Timothy screaming hysterically in his arms. Cloe sat on the sofa, watching the doctor swear and yell at the top of his lungs. He'd been calling everyone he could, but no one had answers for him. Cloe wanted to console the doctor, but things had changed between them since that night at their home, and she felt the very sound of her voice would make things worse. The best she could do was come out of her room, sit on the couch, and hope her presence could be some level of support. However, by the way he purposely ignored her, her assumptions were way off.

Feeling useless, Cloe walked into the kitchen to make her something quick to eat while leaving the panicked doctor alone with his wailing son. Li'l Timothy's screams felt like sonic daggers as they tore through the air, piercing Cloe's calm. She could barely make her sandwich, and the butter knife repeatedly slipped out of her hands each time Timothy's cries invaded her ears. Grunting, Cloe decided to grab something to drink instead and retreat to her room.

I fucking hate kids.

Daniel continued to swear and storm around the villa with Timothy in his arms, and Cloe discovered that unless she did something about the screaming brat, even retreating into her room wouldn't protect her from the child's caterwauls. Closing her eyes and breathing slowly, Cloe deliberately walked over to Daniel and said, "Give me the baby. He shouldn't hear you talk like that."

The sound of Cloe's voice caused Daniel's head to turn so abruptly, Cloe thought his neck would snap in half.

"What did you just say to me?" he asked with rage-filled curiosity in his eyes.

Cloe's eyebrows lifted as she looked up directly into Daniel's eyes and responded, "I said, give me the baby.

He shouldn't hear you cursing like that. That's why he's screaming at the top of his lungs. Let me take him so that you can do what you got to do."

And toss him over the balcony so he will shut the fuck up, Cloe thought as she held out her hands to take Timothy from Daniel. Daniel looked down at Cloe's welcoming arms and momentarily pulled away. Just then, the sound of the president's voice on the phone calling his name forced him to hand his only son over. Timothy's screams intensified as soon as he found himself in Cloe's arms, and he fought with all his strength to free himself from her cold arms. Cloe forced a smile as she held the child tightly in her arms and started walking toward the sliding doors leading out to the balcony.

"No! Don't go out on the balcony. There's no telling how much danger we are in, and I don't want my son or you becoming easy targets," Daniel warned. He then placed the cell phone to his ear to hear what Patrick had to say.

"Hello? Patrick? Are you still there?"

"Yes, Doctor Bennett, I am here."

The solemn tone of the president's voice alarmed Daniel, and he bit down on his bottom lip, trying to keep himself from yelling into the phone.

"Do you have any news on my wife?"

Breathing forcefully, Patrick responded, "Doctor, I won't lie to you. You should prepare yourself for bad news. We haven't heard any new information about the whereabouts of your wife and her companion, but we will be sending troops to Jonglei in the morning to calm the riots in Bor."

"The morning? No, you need to send troops tonight— right now. My wife could still be alive."

"Doctor, you are in no position to order me to do anything. Like I've already told you, prepare for bad news. But I won't risk my soldiers' lives for one woman, even if she is my running mate, and the people love her. I have an entire country to run. You simply have a family. I'm sorry to be the bearer of bad news, Doctor, but these are the realities we face."

"My wife . . ." Daniel paused and clenched his fist, digging his nails into his palms until they punctured flesh. "My wife . . . left here with you. I left my wife in your care because you assured me you would keep her safe during your campaign. Now you're telling me *we* are facing realities? No, motherfuc . . . no, President Djeng. *My son and I* are facing realities. You, on the other hand, will have to face *me*."

"Wait, are you threatening me, Doctor Bennett?"

"I'm just giving you *your* realities if my wife isn't found alive and well."

"Doctor, I'm going to let your threat go as the ramblings of a man in pain. But I will not be so lenient the next time you threaten me. This isn't America, and I'm not *your* president. This is Africa, and we deal with things differently in this part of the world. Remember that the next time you feel inclined to threaten another head of state."

Exhaling, Daniel responded, "Patrick . . . I-I-I'm sorry. I didn't mean—"

"Goodbye, Doctor."

"Wait, Patrick, please—"

"Goodbye, Doctor."

Suddenly, the phone went silent, leaving Daniel standing in the middle of the room in a petrified trance. The tomblike silence spoke louder to him than any sonic boom, and he immediately started to look for Cloe and Li'l Timothy.

"Cloe? Timothy?"

The longer he called out to Cloe and his son, the more he began to panic, and within minutes, he was sprinting throughout the large villa like a madman. Goose bumps started to cover his skin, and a nasty lump began to grow in his throat as his yells turned to screams of terror and desperation. His screams alerted the lieutenant and his men, and they quickly rushed into the villa with their guns raised and safeties off. Lieutenant Ruiz held up his hand, ordering his men to stand still as he watched Daniel run from one end of the villa to the next. As much as Lieutenant Ruiz wanted to separate himself from the anguish and terror that was choking the air, he couldn't, and he decided to try to calm his employer down to get to the bottom of what was going on.

"Mr. Bennett, Mr. Bennett, how can we help?"

"My son . . . My son is gone. He isn't here. He was just here. She was holding him, and she was going out to the . . . oh my God, no," Daniel whimpered as he sprinted outside on the balcony. It didn't take long for the lieutenant to understand precisely what was going on and shook his head in shame.

"I want everyone to secure this location and find that baby and woman—now," Ruiz ordered, and his men didn't hesitate to spring into action. The lieutenant then followed Daniel out onto the balcony to get more details from the hysterical doctor.

"Timothy! Timothy!" Daniel screamed out into the night, praying the beautiful sound of his son's voice would cry out to him, assuring him that he was safe. The only thing he got in return was the harsh sound of the lieutenant's voice, asking him to explain how Cloe and his son vanished into thin air. Daniel turned around, looked the lieutenant up and down, and said, "That's a question *you* should be answering—*not* me. I paid you a great deal of money for you and your men to keep my family and me safe, and so far, we've had an assassin share a bath with my wife, and now, my son and Cloe are missing—all under *your* watch."

"Mr. Bennett, I don't kno—"

"Lieutenant, the last thing I need from anyone right now is another 'I don't know,'" Daniel responded, leaning forward on the balcony railing. "My wife is out there somewhere with a trained killer and an entire state of people that want her dead. Now, my son is missing. I'm losing everything that matters to me, and the last thing I need is another person telling me they don't know something. I just want to know. Can you find my family and bring them back to me alive?"

Daniel felt his throat drying and his lungs burning in his chest. He felt as if there were an invisible hand inside his chest, squeezing his heart and causing him lots of pain. Suddenly, the world seemed to lose focus and the night's lights started to blend as tears began to fall down his face. The muscles in his arms and legs were shaking as if he'd just been hit with thousands of volts of electricity. The lieutenant watched Daniel slowly fall to his knees, moaning loudly while holding himself, as if he were afraid he would literally fall to pieces. Covering his mouth with his hand, the lieutenant looked away from the weeping doctor, trying his best not to be sucked in by his pain. The doctor's suffering was so personal that the lieutenant felt his emotional gates slowly open, and then suddenly, a tap on the shoulder saved him.

"Sir, we have looked over the entire property, and there are no signs of the woman or the doctor's son."

"Any signs of where the intruder may have entered the villa?"

"No sir, not even tracks leading away from the house after the abduction."

Whoever did this is just as good as John Smith. Fuck me.

"Okay, secure the house and wait for further instructions."

"Yes, sir."

"Doctor Bennett, I'm sorry, but we have to start preparing for the reality that we may soon be receiving a call demanding something in return for your son and Cloe's life. Money isn't the only motivation for these people, so their demands could mean trading someone else's life for theirs. Whatever their plans are, they won't stop until they complete them. I'll leave you alone for a minute."

"No, I don't need to be left alone. I need a gun, some gear, and some intel. I will no longer stay on my knees. They couldn't have gotten far, and seeing how they were able to get in and out of this villa undetected shows they know this terrain very well, so wherever they are holding them, it isn't far from here."

The look of shock on the lieutenant's face was nothing compared to the look of rage and hatred in Daniel's eyes. Things had started to become more apparent to him as he was on his knees. He understood that everything that's happened, including Li'l Timothy's abduction, wasn't a coincidence or a series of unfortunate events. Even the fact where they were living seemed to be one of the many pieces set up by someone who was always several steps ahead of him. No matter what he did, he was always playing someone else's game. It was time for him to be unpredictable. Rising to his feet, Daniel walked over to Lieutenant Ruiz, looked him directly in his eyes, and said, "It's time to put your training to the test, Lieutenant."

"Mr. Bennett, I don't think trying to go after these people is a good idea. These are highly trained assassins."

"And you and your men are highly trained soldiers. If we can't find and rescue my 3-year-old son, then what the fuck are you doing here? Why do you proudly wear the emblem of the Navy SEALs?"

"We're not here as Navy SEALs. We are here as mercenaries. Big difference, Mr. Bennett."

"So, you're not going with me?"

"I didn't say that. Of course, we're going with you. I just wanted you to understand the waters we'll be treading, completely, sir."

"Duly noted."

"And you're still gonna do this, I assume?"

"He's my son, Lieutenant."

"Very well, we move out in fifteen. I will leave four men behind to secure this location and be in place in case your wife and John return while we are on the mission. The rest of us will be going in weapons-free. Now, Doctor Bennett, I need a few minutes to contact a few people so I can get satellite imaging of this location over the last two hours to pinpoint where the kidnappers could be holding up."

"No problem. Anything you need from me?"

The lieutenant looked Daniel up and down and responded, "I need for you to get your head in the game and stay frosty. I don't need you going rogue once we get in the thick of things. Am I making myself clear, sir?"

"Crystal."

"Good, we move out in thirteen. Prepare."

Chapter Thirteen

Driving Mrs. Bennett

Somewhere on the outskirts of Bor
South Sudan

The pitch darkness seemed to magnify her anxiety as Ayana leaned against an old military Jeep. Meanwhile, John was under the hood, trying to get the relic to come back to life to save theirs. Each time he fiddled around inside the Jeep's guts, he caused its metal innards to protest with loud, position-revealing noises. Ayana cringed every time the sharp sound of colliding metal echoed in the night, and she frequently looked around, praying no one was close enough to hear them. Gripping the AK-47 tightly in her hands, she leaned toward the side of the Jeep and peered around it to make sure no one was attempting to flank them, but the blinding darkness prevented her from seeing more than a few feet ahead of her. Wiping the mixture of blood and sweat from her forehead, Ayana moved back to her previous position and leaned against the side of the Jeep again, waiting for John to finish.

John would periodically grunt in frustration as he fumbled around under the small light of Ayana's cell phone. Although he was surrounded by metal and the loud, clanking sounds of him carrying out his task, John was still attentive to his surroundings and could hear and smell everything. He knew Ayana was on high alert due to the lack of visibility, but the darkness was a welcome ally for John. He smiled and quickly climbed into the driver's seat after connecting a few more wires and tubes. He played around with the ignition, then the Jeep's exhaust barked loudly while spewing black fumes into the air. Ayana's eyes widened as the rumbling of the vehicle's resurrected engine caught her by surprise. She never thought John would be able to get it started, and the fact he did . . . very impressive.

Jumping to her feet, she slammed the hood shut and climbed into the passenger seat next to John. Once he knew she was secured, he pulled off down the dark, winding road of their escape. Still holding on to her assault rifle, Ayana looked around and then glanced over at John as he calmly drove through the night with the headlights off.

How the hell can he see?

Noticing her secret curiosity, John turned and looked at Ayana and asked, "What is it, love?"

"Nothing," she responded while turning away her gaze.

"No, no. Don't be shy. What is it?"

Exhaling forcefully, Ayana responded, "Is there any-thing you *can't* do?"

"I'm not sure. I haven't come across it yet. I'll surely let you know if I do."

Sucking her teeth, Ayana adjusted her body so that her back was turned to him. Noticing her reaction, John chuckled and returned his attention to the road. After nearly a minute, Ayana couldn't contain herself and asked, "Do you always have to be such a dick?"

"I kill people for a living, love. I think being a dick is one of my more redeeming qualities."

Ayana's body suddenly went cold once the gravity of John's words sank in. She'd been so caught up in the day's violence and adrenaline rush that she'd forgotten she had been gallivanting alone in the dark with a highly trained killer. Her anxiety alarmed John, and he quickly reached over and held her hand, looked her in the eyes, and said, "I would never hurt you or let anyone else hurt you."

The two of them stared into each other's eyes as the Jeep continued to speed forward in the darkness. The open top of the vehicle allowed the night breeze to blow through Ayana's dreads, and John's heart skipped a beat as he marveled at her beauty, even while covered in blood and dirt from the day's earlier carnage.

My God, what is she doing to me?

Ayana stared into John's blue eyes and saw compassion, something she didn't believe was possible from a killer like him. Her hand in his sent tingles and warmth through her, and she began to feel safe and secure, a feeling that's been missing for too long. Suddenly, from the corner of her eye, Ayana saw the rear lights of a vehicle getting dangerously close, and she screamed out just before John snapped out of his trance. Snatching the steering wheel to the left, the Jeep swerved and jerked, violently tossing Ayana on top of John's lap. His eyes swelled with excitement as he said, "Oh, Mrs. Bennett, there's only one passenger per seat on this ride."

There goes that dick again. Good, 'cause I was losing my mind a few seconds ago.

Ayana quickly climbed out of his lap and started to fasten her seat belt, but John's hand reached over again to stop her. Looking down at his hand wrapped around her wrist, Ayana shook her head and said, "John, listen, I'm not—"

"Later for that, love, we have company," he responded while drawing her attention to the rearview mirror. Ayana turned around and watched as the headlights of the truck they almost hit drew closer. Before she could say anything, the flash and loud pop of automatic gunfire erupted around them. Ayana ducked in her seat just before her entire headrest was torn to pieces by gunfire. She looked over at John for answers, and the assassin playfully shrugged his shoulders and said, "I can't shoot and drive, love. I'm not 007. You're gonna have to handle our guests while I drive this piece-of-shit Jeep."

Ayana's lips retreated into her mouth as she nodded her head while silently promising payback. She then closed her eyes and took a deep breath, attempting to calm her nerves and prepare herself to stick her head up and into the path of gunfire. Noticing what she was about to do, John shook his head and said, "Haven't you noticed they haven't fired a single shot since you've been hiding behind your chair? I think it's best if you return fire from between the front seats and take out the truck driver. That's what I would do, but I'm no one but the best there is. So . . ."

Rolling her eyes so hard the motion gave her a momentary headache, Ayana responded, "I think labeling being a dick as a redeeming quality is a false advertisement at best, John." She then rolled over and began to return fire at the truck behind them. The front glass of the truck shattered as her bullets penetrated the front cab of the truck. Their pursuers immediately returned fire, and John veered to the right to avoid a hail of bullets that would've torn him to pieces.

"That was close," he said playfully.

Ayana glanced over at him with a confused look on her face while thinking, *Why is he entertained?*

She peeked between the seats to get a better view of the driver, and suddenly, a low thumping sound filled her ears. As she glanced in the backseat, the light from the truck's headlights allowed her to see the grenade rolling on the floor in the back of the Jeep. Gasping, Ayana reached out, grabbed the grenade, and tossed it over the side of the Jeep just before it exploded, sending a concussive blast of heat, fire, and metal fragments everywhere. The force of the explosion pushed the Jeep off its right-side wheels, almost tipping them over.

"What the fuck are you doing?" John yelled at her, as he frantically maneuvered the Jeep back down on all four of its wheels. "Next time, why don't you toss the grenade *behind* us so that maybe it can take out our guests? You think that could be a better strategy?"

"Fuck you, John."

Name the place and time, and I'll show you another reason why they say I'm the best.

The smile and blissful look that appeared on John's face gave Ayana an idea of precisely what he was thinking, and she frowned aggressively.

"You're unbelievable."

"Whatever. Enough chatter. Guns, bullets behind us. Get rid of our guests, please."

Gritting her teeth, Ayana aimed her gun at the truck, and after releasing two short bursts of gunfire into the truck's cabin, the truck began to swerve behind them. Noticing she hit her target, she continued to fire at the vehicle until the engine erupted into flames. Ayana watched with great satisfaction as the truck suddenly exploded, tearing it and its passengers to pieces of hot metal and burning flesh. Turning around and returning to what was left of her seat, Ayana looked over at John with pride. He tried his best to pretend he wasn't impressed, but he couldn't hide his reverence for her.

"That was an exhilarating experience. Now that playtime's over, let's get you back home safely, love, shall we?"

After several hours of driving, John suddenly turned on the headlights, just when they were passing the sign indicating that they were leaving the state of Jonglei, and Ayana's body immediately relaxed as she sighed while closing her eyes. Having the relaxed mind to think clearly, she looked over at John and said, "Thank you, John, for saving my life today."

"No need to thank me. It was fun, and I had a bit of help as well," he responded with a sly smirk on his face. "I had no idea you were such a ferocious killer, Mrs. Bennett. I'm impressed."

"I'm not a killer."

"Oh, I beg to differ. Your years with that degenerate bastard, Kronte, has turned you into an incredible creature indeed."

"John, if this is your attempt at a compliment, you're failing miserably."

"Don't take it personally, love. I'm serious when I tell you I'm impressed, and very few people impress me."

"Didn't Kronte impress you?"

"What? God, no. He was a steaming pile of shit that only served a purpose, and once his usefulness was exhausted, he was discarded."

"What makes you any different? You work for the same people he did."

"Nothing, to be brutally honest, love. Well, besides I'm a lot easier on the eyes."

Rolling her eyes, Ayana responded, "And you're okay with that?"

"Of course, love. Why wouldn't I want to be a beautiful man?"

Uugh. This man is working my nerves.

"John, focus. I wasn't talking about your looks."

"Oh, that. I'm merely a pawn in the grand scheme of things—nothing I can do about it. I learned a long time ago, there's no winning against the people I work for. Well, used to work for."

"Used to?"

"Yes, after today's fiasco, I'm sure they are now aware of my involvement in your miraculous escape from the clutches of death back at your home in the US."

"But we demanded no cameras or press at that debate. How could they know of your involvement?"

"Because they had a man in place."

"Who?"

"Asim."

"Wait. What? Asim works for your people?"

"Yes. They enlisted his allegiance a little over three years ago."

"Three years? That's around the time when—"

"Uh-huh . . . exactly."

Ayana's eyes widened as a revelation took over her. The shock and revelation of what John revealed to her were terrifying.

"Asim killed Kronte?"

"Yes, he and his men decided to take the contract, with the promise of one day ruling this country themselves."

"What? How can they promise that?"

"Come on, love. Do you actually think Africa, or any country for that matter, makes their own decisions? You are a former high-ranking United Nations delegate. You know better than most how things go in this world. My employers are the ones that make the rules, and everyone else follows them."

"But once upon a time, you didn't feel the way you do now, correct?"

"How's that?"

"Well, you said earlier that you learned a long time ago that there's no winning against whoever you work or used to work for. That leads me to believe that before you became the man you are today, you fought against them."

"I was a different man back then, foolish and unaware of the 'what could happen' if I joined the losing side."

John's entire demeanor changed, his aura of confidence broke down, and Ayana felt a deep and engaging sense of regret fill the air. Looking at John's empty gaze, she suddenly understood that John had a past so full of loss and pain that he decided to work for the very people that caused it.

What did those people do to him?

Glancing over at Ayana, John noticed her look of compassion, and he quickly came back to himself. Ayana's eyes almost popped out of her head when she watched his expression transform from a man to a cold-blooded killer in less than a second. As an expert in human behavior, she knew exactly the kind of psychosis the assassin was suffering from, and she decided to tread lightly before he decided to protect the mental island he'd marooned himself on to hide away from his pain.

"I don't need your pity, love. I made my choices a long time ago. It's too late for either of us."

"Excuse me?"

Turning and giving Ayana a sarcastic grin, John responded, "You enjoy killing; you enjoy the rush and power it gives you when you take a life. The way you viciously fought your way out of that building earlier was just . . . well . . . almost erotic. You don't become that efficient in taking a life unless you enjoy it. Trust me. I know."

"I did what I had to do to get back to my family."

"Bull-fucking-shit, Mrs. Bennett. You are already plotting your escape from the good doctor, and being a single mother is not a 'family.' Sorry to disappoint, but it's true. Americans tend to believe one-parent households are all the rave, but in actuality, it's a failure of the most basic rule of life."

"And what's that?"

"Always have backup."

"You don't understand what I've gone through—what I'm still going through."

"You're preaching to the choir, Mrs. Bennett. I understand but don't pretend you didn't enjoy what we had to do today. You are a predator, *not* the prey."

"Don't presume to think you know me, Assassin."

"I don't presume anything. You are right, I don't know you, but I would love to explore every single inch of who you are."

John's words sent a tingling sensation through Ayana's body as she imagined exactly what he meant by "every inch." Pressing her legs together and folding her arms over her chest, Ayana remained silent. She started looking out the Jeep's window, attempting to expel the images of John exploring her with the same skill he dispatched people to the afterlife.

I am in so much trouble.

Chapter Fourteen

Do Not Breach

One hour later
Juba, South Sudan

Daniel moved through the African bush with Lieutenant Ruiz and eleven of his men behind him. Before leaving the villa, the lieutenant made it clear that Daniel would be taking the point since he was adamant about searching for the kidnappers' base of operations. The lieutenant had hoped making the doctor take the lead would discourage him from going on this suicide mission, but when the lieutenant ordered him to take point, Daniel didn't hesitate. They'd been searching the area for almost two hours, and Daniel couldn't find any signs of his son's abductors.

The lieutenant was becoming impatient as the night dragged on and decided to cancel the mission until Daniel stopped in front of them, raised an open hand, and closed it quickly. Everyone immediately took cover as Daniel began to crawl on all fours toward what appeared to be a large, abandoned building. Using the night vision scope on his assault rifle, Daniel looked over the outside of the building and noticed it seemed to be an unfinished luxury hotel development. The entire parking lot was overgrown with foliage, and all the windows on the front of the building were shattered or gaping holes of darkness. Daniel couldn't see any movements behind the shattered windows, but something told him this is where they were keeping his son.

Backing away from his point of observation, Daniel joined the rest of the team and began to give them his assessment of the building. After explaining the condition of the hotel, advantages, and disadvantages of the surrounding terrain, the lieutenant, apparently impressed with Daniel's expert assessment, nodded his head and signaled for everyone to follow him to the hotel. The group of men, wearing all-black uniforms and night vision goggles, crept toward the outskirts of the hotel's parking lot. They took position along the tree line facing the front of the hotel and awaited instructions from the lieutenant. Without saying a word, the lieutenant signaled the team to split up and take up positions in front and behind the hotel.

The lieutenant ordered Daniel to stay with him, and the two men joined the team that would move in from the rear of the building. The journey through the brush was slow, and Daniel was anxious to get inside the structure before they were discovered, and the kidnappers moved his son to another location. After a five-minute trip that seemed like five hours, Daniel, Lieutenant Ruiz, and the other four men that accompanied them were bent down in the thick brush in the back of the building, awaiting further orders. Lieutenant Ruiz surveyed the building through the night vision scope on his weapon, and once he was satisfied no one was observing them, he ordered everyone to move inside the building. The men immediately began running toward the hotel's loading dock. Because there wasn't a door on the dock's entrance, the men jumped up on the dock's platform and quickly moved inside while carefully checking their corners.

The men's movements were fluid and synchronized like a well-rehearsed ballet of war as they moved in the dark hallways of the abandoned building. The air inside the building was thick with the rancid odor of mildew and feces. Once the burn of the stench flooded Daniel's nose, he held his breath to hold back the vomit that was threatening to erupt out of his mouth. The other men didn't seem bothered by the odor as they continued to move through each room of the ground floor, looking for signs of life. The men that came in through the front were already moving up toward the second floor, and a few times, the sound of their footsteps above his head made Daniel jump and point his weapon above his head.

Eventually, the men came to the stairwell leading to the second floor, and Ruiz paused for a few seconds before he began slowly moving up the stairs. Daniel and the other four men followed behind him, alert and ready for anything. They eventually made it to the second floor, while the other team was already moving on the third floor.

Throughout their journey in the building, Daniel noticed that none of the rooms had doors on them, and walking past each opening made him grimace at the thought of being ambushed by a hail of bullets. Suddenly, the voice of one of the men on the third floor came through the communication devices in their ears, and everyone took defensive positions along the long hallway of the second floor.

"Sir, we have movement and sounds of a young boy crying on the third floor behind a locked door. We are in position and are going to breach in five, four, three, two . . ."

A locked door? Ruiz thought. Suddenly, his eyes widened as a thought hit him like an aluminum bat.

"Soldier, do not breach that—"

It felt as if the Four Horsemen of the Apocalypse had descended on the building as the entire upper levels of the hotel exploded in fire and concrete. The massive quake shook the building to its foundation and tossed the men on the second floor around like leaves in the wind. The building started to crumble and burn around them, and Ruiz quickly jumped to his feet and snatched a semiconscious Daniel to his feet.

"We have to get out of here now!" Ruiz yelled over the roar of destruction that was unraveling around them. Still trying to regain himself after the explosion, Daniel nodded his head, and the two men started to stumble toward the staircase. The other four men quickly jumped to their feet and ran past Daniel and the lieutenant toward the stairs, leaving them behind. Daniel was moving painstakingly slow, but Ruiz refused to leave him, so he threw his arm around his shoulders, allowing him to brace his weight up against him. Daniel stumbled forward and noticed the other men sprinting down the stairs and shook his head.

Fucking cowards.

Suddenly, the entire concrete ceiling above the staircase shifted and collapsed, smashing the men that were on the stairwell running for safety. The lieutenant cringed as his men's screams echoed above the booming sound of the building falling to pieces. Daniel, on the other hand, wasn't moved by their cries of agony.

Leave no man behind. Remember that shit?

Regaining his composure, Daniel lifted himself up, and the two men looked down at the crumpled heap of death, steel, and fire that continued to burn on the first floor. Both men concluded within seconds that they would have to find an alternative way out of the crumbling building before it became their final resting place.

Running toward the other side of the hotel, Daniel and the lieutenant raced toward an opening as the floors and ceiling crumbled around them. The closer they got to the window, the more the falling building tried to stop them, but both men scrambled, jumped, clawed, and climbed their way closer to the salvation of the open air outside.

"Go, go, go, go, goooo!" Ruiz screamed at Daniel as he dove out of a second-floor window, with the lieutenant right behind him. The contact with the ground was not kind or subtle, and the intense pain trembled throughout their bodies as they rolled and moaned. Suddenly, Daniel jumped to his feet and began screaming his son's name, as the building fell in on itself. Daniel raised his hands in the air, screaming and panting, driven insane with grief. The lieutenant helplessly watched as Daniel lost his sanity, and it tore him to pieces. He'd failed to keep the doctor's family and most of his team members alive, men who he'd known and trusted for years. Nevertheless, this wasn't the place or time for mourning the dead. They were out in the open, vulnerable, and exposed.

"Doctor Bennett, we have to go. We have to go *now*."

Daniel stopped screaming his son's name and closed his eyes as the lieutenant's words filled his ears. He didn't want to leave, but he knew Ruiz was right, and it made no sense to die here before getting the answers he needed. Nodding his head, Daniel turned around as if in a trance and began a slow, zombielike stroll back toward the villa, as the realization of losing another child in the same country came crashing down on him. His overwhelming grief burned him, and he knew he was to blame—all because he didn't listen.

Had I just waited for the kidnappers to make their demands like Ruiz advised, Timothy might still be alive. Just like Victoria . . . Had I just listened, she would still

*be alive. I don't deserve to live, and as soon as I find out
if my wife is alive or dead, I'm going to rid this world of
my useless life. Timmy . . . my God . . . my son.*

Several hours later, Daniel and Lieutenant Ruiz walked
up to the villa, and Daniel immediately noticed the
run-down military Jeep parked out front. The lieutenant
stepped in front of Daniel, holding him at bay as he studied the countless bullet holes and damage to the Jeep. He
then walked toward the front and placed his hands on
the hood of the vehicle.

Still warm.

He then looked around for the four men he'd left
behind to guard the villa, but there were no signs of them.

Where are my other men?

Signaling two fingers toward his eyes and then pointing toward the front door, Ruiz and Daniel quietly
approached the villa and stood on either side of the
threshold. Counting down with his left hand until he
reached "one," Ruiz kicked open the front door, and the
two of them rushed into the villa with their guns raised,
ready to fire. At that very moment, Ayana strolled out
of the bathroom, dripping wet in just a bath towel, with
John Smith directly behind her, pulling up his zipper
with his belt and pants undone. He was breathing heavily
and shirtless, exposing his well-defined muscular chest,
drenched in sweat or water. Daniel couldn't tell which,
because at that moment, all he saw was red as he stormed
across the room toward John. John watched Daniel rush
toward him and smiled as he waited for him to get within
striking distance.

Growling like a wild beast, Daniel swung wildly at
John's head, and John quickly stepped back and to the
side. With Daniel out of position and John standing be-

side him, John struck Daniel with a strong straight right to his jaw. Daniel quickly swung his right arm backward, attempting to hit back, but John quickly ducked under his swing and came up with a devastating uppercut. Daniel's body lifted in the air and came crashing down onto the hard marble floor. Despite the intense pain, he immediately jumped to his feet and tried to attack John again. John calmly stepped back and struck Daniel with a right and left hook that sent him back down to the floor. Still undeterred by the pain or spinning room, Daniel was back up on his feet again, this time with a mouth full of blood from the deep cuts John's strikes opened in his mouth.

Daniel leaped forward with a powerful front kick. John quickly twisted his body to the side, and once Daniel's kick soared past him, John then turned toward Daniel, and with his left arm raised, he jolted forward and clotheslined Daniel by the throat, sending him flying backward onto the floor again. This time, the back of Daniel's head cracked once it collided with the marble floor. Daniel's vision became blurred as he felt the wet and warm thickness of his blood run out of his head and onto the floor like a river. Screaming, Daniel stumbled to his feet, and despite his legs struggling to keep him standing, he continued to attack John. Amused and aggravated, John continued to beat Daniel within an inch of his life.

During the beginning of their confrontation, Ayana watched with great satisfaction. She wanted Daniel to suffer for his betrayal, and there was no better person to exact justice than John. The lieutenant, on the other hand, watched with concern, but his hands were tied. He knew trying to assist Daniel in attacking the assassin could mean his own death as well as Ayana's, so he decided to stand down and hope the good doctor could either get the best of John or come to his senses and stop. As the savage beating continued, Ayana's satisfied smile slowly transformed into a frown as watching Daniel being beaten to death started to tear her apart. Soon her fear turned to terror as Daniel continued to come after John, who happily obliged him by beating him to a bloody pulp.

"Why do you continue to fight?" John antagonized, while he continued to beat Daniel to the punch each time that he tried to hit the assassin.

"Stop it! That's enough," Ayana screamed, but the two men ignored her. "Aren't you gonna do something? Where's your team?" Ayana yelled at the lieutenant, who grimaced in regret when Ayana's question reminded him he was now in this mess alone. Ayana rushed over to John to stop him, but before she could reach him, he turned and looked back at her with the eyes of a murderer. Holding up his index finger, he waved it from side to side, as his attention was momentarily taken away from Daniel. The coldness in his eyes froze her in place, and without looking at Daniel, who was barely standing, he struck him across the head with a swinging right kick that sent him reeling to the floor. Exhausted, beaten, and bleeding profusely, Daniel lay on the floor, coughing uncontrollably as he choked on his own blood. John continued to stare at Ayana with disapproving eyes, and when he started to move toward her, the lieutenant immediately raised his weapon and aimed it at John.

"Stay away from her. If you touch her, I will—"

"Mind your words, Lieutenant. I warned you before about threatening my li—"

Without warning, John's feet were pulled from under him, and he fell backward onto the floor. The collision with the floor knocked the wind out of the assassin, and before he could recover, Daniel was on top of him, raining down haymaker after haymaker. Daniel attacked

John like a rabid gorilla, pounding John's head with all the strength his injured body had left in it. John's face quickly began to cut, swell, and bruise as the assault continued until Daniel was so exhausted, he collapsed on top of him. Coughing and gasping from the blood that poured out of his eyes, nose, and mouth, John tried to get up, but his body was spent. Inhaling deeply, Daniel grabbed John by his throat and began to squeeze until he could see the assassin's skin turning blue under all the crimson liquid that covered his face.

Leaning in closer, Daniel said, "I will *never* stop fighting for her. I would die for her. Are *you* willing to die for her?"

Chuckling while spitting out blood from his mouth, John smiled, revealing a mouth full of bloodstained teeth, and replied, "Now that I've tasted her, I would be inclined to say, yes."

A perfectly placed head butt wiped the smile from John's face as his eyes rolled to the back of his head, and he slowly lost consciousness. Ayana knelt next to Daniel, placed her soft, warm hands on his shoulder, and asked, "Daniel, where's Timmy? Where's our son?"

Daniel turned and looked at her, and through the bloodstained slits of what used to be his eyes, she saw the answer to her question, and she gasped in horror. Shaking her head wildly, she searched Daniel's face for any sign of salvation from the oncoming agony, but he offered none. Daniel closed his eyes, rolled over on the floor, and began to weep. Ayana slowly stood up and turned to look at the lieutenant, but he looked down at the floor, too ashamed to tell a mother that her 3-year-old boy was dead.

A cry of agony escaped her lips as she ran through the house screaming her son's name, hoping someone had made a mistake. Unfortunately, after looking in every room, under every bed, and in every closet, she discovered that her baby wasn't there. Stumbling back into the living area, Ayana braced her body against the wall, trying to stop the room from spinning. Soon, her hand began to slip, and she eventually collapsed onto the floor, screaming while tearing at the white towel wrapped around her body. Watching the parents grieve caused Ruiz's ironclad resolve to fold, and his legs gave way as he slid down onto the floor, shaking and weeping at the events of the day that led to the death of his team and an innocent, 3-year-old boy.

Chapter Fifteen

Is This the End?

Five hours later
Chicago, Illinois

Timothy looked up at the ceiling of his condo, lying next to several empty bottles of vodka while contemplating mass murder or suicide. He'd been crying and drinking for hours, and after drinking bottle after bottle of expensive vodka, his professional diagnosis was surely alcohol poisoning. Moaning, he rolled over on his side and tried to pour the remaining vodka into his mouth, but he missed and poured it all over the expensive hardwood flooring.

"Shit," he muttered as he tried to right the bottle's angle but only managed to pour vodka all over his face this time. The liquid burned his eyes, and he snatched away from the bottle and rolled over on the opposite side. Struggling to sit up, Timothy slid back onto the floor and kicked wildly in frustration at his drunken awkwardness. The tears started to fall again once his godson's beautiful and innocent face flashed through his mind, and he rolled over onto his stomach, screaming into the floor until his throat was raw.

A loud knock on the door silenced Timothy's screams of agony, and he rolled over on his back and yelled, "Go away. Can't you leave a grieving man in peace?"

"Timothy? It's me."

Her sweet and sultry voice startled him as his intoxicated mind tried to place the voice with the person on the other side of the door. His pain yearned for Meagan, but the longer the woman called out his name, he accepted it wasn't her at his door. Instead, the voice belonged to Mrs. Karlov, his ex and "Queen Tease a Dick" extraordinaire. Frowning, Timothy decided to ignore her until she got the message, but after nearly ten minutes of banging, he concluded that Simone wouldn't leave until he let her in.

Forcing himself to his feet, Timothy stumbled to the front door. As he staggered past the living room couch, his left leg hit the end table, sending him falling to the hard floor on his face. Swearing loudly, Timothy lifted himself up while rocking and swaying his body until he was back up on his feet. Deciding it was best to balance himself against something, Timothy dragged his body against the wall until he made his way to the front door. Inhaling deeply while rolling his neck, he unlocked the front door and swung it open. The cold air from the outside hallway hit him like a miniature blizzard, and suddenly, his vision began to fade.

The water was a raging beast as the thundering black sky was split with the blinding cuts of lightning. He could hear his cries in the darkness, calling out his name. His arms were weak and felt like overcooked noodles, trying to keep his 210-pound frame afloat. As he inhaled, the mist of the salt water rushed into his mouth and down his throat, burning the sensitive skin like liquid fire. He could hear him in the dark, just a few more feet now. The ocean continued to protest with each crashing wave, hitting him with such force that he thought he would be taken under for good each time.

His voice, his sweet, innocent voice, screamed in terror in the darkness of this hurricane on the open sea. Suddenly, he saw him, his dark, curly hair, and his hazel eyes like his mother's were wide with terror, but when he saw him, a hint of hope shined in them. It was that tiny hope that gave him the strength and determination he needed to swim and fight harder against the raging sea.

He could see him, the flashing lights from the lightning, giving him a clear view of his objective. Suddenly, a large flash of light lit up the entire area, and that's when he saw it—a dark tsunami rolling in from behind him as he waited to be saved. He tried to scream, to warn him, but nothing came out of his mouth. The monster of aquatic destruction continued to roar closer, and as fast as he tried to get to the boy, the tsunami was moving faster. It was directly behind the child, casting an evil shadow that made him turn around just in time to see it surging down on him.

"Timothy! Noooo!"

Timothy's body jumped as he swung his arms and legs, trying to keep himself afloat. Simone leaned backward to avoid being hit and wet while trying to calm him down.

"Timothy, it's okay. You're just having a nightmare. You're fine. I got you, baby. I got you."

Timothy's eyes shot open, and once his eyes got used to the change of lighting, he discovered he was at home in his own soaker tub . . . completely naked. Shocked, he quickly turned around to see Simone kneeling next to the tub, looking at him with grave concern that made goose bumps pop up all over his arms and back. Looking away from her sorrowed gaze, Timothy wiped the warm water from his face and asked, "What are you doing here, and why am I naked?"

"I'm here to help you. When you opened the door, you passed out on the floor. You could've killed yourself with all the alcohol you consumed. The world needs you, Timmy. You can't just up and drink yourself to death."

"You don't know what you're talking about. But you still haven't answered my question. Why are you here?"

Sighing gently while running her soft hands through his hair, Simone responded, "I heard about Li'l Timothy, and I wanted to check on you to make sure you were okay."

"Wait a minute. How did you kno—"

"Shhhh. Rest. You need to rest," Simone responded while massaging his scalp and the back of his neck. Timothy's eyes rolled in his head as Simone's experienced hands brought him an unparalleled amount of relaxing pleasure. His body and mind quickly submitted as Simone continued to console his scalp and neck. Thirty minutes later, Timothy slowly strolled out of the bathroom, and his nose was immediately bombarded with the smell of curry.

Indian? She remembered, he thought, as he walked over to his dining room table that was covered in his favorite cuisine.

"You know I'm not known for my cooking, so I hope you don't mind me getting takeout."

"Yeah, cooking was never one of your strong points," he responded sarcastically. "Knowing boundaries is something that escapes you as well."

"Tim, let's not go there. You know you wanted me in that elevator just as much as I wanted you. Let's not pretend—"

"Umm, I'm not talking about the elevator tease. I'm talking about showing up here at my home, unannounced and uninvited, stripping me butt-ass naked, and bathing me."

"*And* a massage," she added.

"Yeah, that too . . . although I rather enjoyed that part . . . but that's beside the point. And how do you even know where I live?"

Giving him a look as if he were an idiot, Simone responded, "Really? Besides the fact my husband gave you a great deal of money, I'm a woman. We fucking know everything."

Nodding, Timothy whispered, "Yeah, you have a point there."

"Tim, I'm not here to complicate things for you. I'm just here because I care, and I wanted to make sure you're okay. Now that I see you are at least alive, I'll leave. I'm sorry for *overstepping* boundaries."

As if that elevator scene didn't shatter boundaries already, she thought as she grabbed her purse and started for the door.

"Simone, wait. I'm sorry. I shouldn't be upset with you. I'm just in a terrible place, and although you were the last person I was expecting to show up at my door, I'm grateful, and I really don't want to eat alone right now. So, would you join me for dinner before you go?"

With her back to him, Simone smiled, shimmied her shoulders, turned around, and almost skipped back to the table. Chuckling at her response, Timothy joined her, and the two of them enjoyed a quiet meal together.

A few days later, Timothy waited in the baggage claim area of O'Hare Airport with heavy and dreadful anticipation. He didn't want to see the wooden box, the pain in his friends' eyes, or suffer the madness of guilt for leaving his friend when he needed him the most. An eager group of reporters suddenly sprang into a frenzy once Daniel, Ayana, and the lieutenant were spotted coming down the escalators. They bombarded them with tough question after tough question while taking pictures and invading their private spaces. Lieutenant Ruiz tried his best to keep them at bay, but Timothy noticed he wasn't the same man he was before he left. His confidence, as well as his entire team, had been taken from him, and he wore his shame like a scarlet letter. Like rabid canines, the reporters could sniff out his lack of confidence, and they ignored his warnings each time they got too close.

I need to handle this before Daniel knocks one of these disrespectful motherfuckers out.

"Back the fuck up. All of you. Can't you see this family is grieving? You'll get your questions answered in due time, but right now, the Bennett family needs privacy and space."

One of the reporters, not intimidated by Timothy's aggression, asked, "And who the hell are you?"

Timothy quickly moved toward the reporter, towering over him while returning the favor of invading *his* private space, and whispered in his ear, "Do you *really* want to know the answer to that question?"

Hearing the aggressive tone in his ear, the reporter swallowed hard and shook his head.

"Good," Timothy said while smiling and patting the reporter on his chest and adjusting his coat's collar. Suddenly, the loud and chaotic chatter of the media died down as everyone watched Timothy intimidate the once-brave reporter.

"Now, ladies and gentlemen, please make a path so we can get out of here. Thank you for your cooperation," Timothy said while escorting his friends and the lieutenant away from the crowd. Once the Bennetts and Ruiz had gathered their belongings, the four of them headed outside to the waiting vehicles, which would transport them to a hotel on the Magnificent Mile in downtown

Chicago. Ayana refused to go back to their old home in Highland Park, and Daniel didn't hesitate to oblige her. No matter what may or may not have happened between her and the assassin, he still loved her, and he was willing to do whatever he had to do to fix their marriage. The ride to the hotel was slow, silent, and uncomfortable, as no one wanted to say anything that could reopen fresh wounds.

After making sure they were checked in, Timothy followed them up to their hotel room and helped them get their bags inside. Ayana retreated to one of the bedrooms, and Ruiz posted himself outside their hotel room door. Daniel and Timothy stood in front of each other in the middle of the living room without saying a word. The silent standoff dragged on until Timothy's lips began to tremble, and his eyes started to flood as he whispered, "I'm so sorry. Oh my God, I'm *so* sorry."

Daniel reached for his friend, and the two men cried as they embraced, each drawing strength from the other. The two weeping men eventually sat on the couch as Daniel buried his head in his hands and said, "I don't want to be here anymore, Tim. I want to be with my son. This world is too cold and violent for me."

"You can't talk like that. Other people are depending on you to keep on living."

"Like whom? Ayana? Even after nearly being beaten to death, she still won't talk or even look at me. Sometimes, I feel like we are two immovable objects that collided, and we are destroying each other. She's known nothing but pain since she's been with me."

"That's not true. You two have shared a love many would envy. I can't believe you think you are no good for each other."

Looking up at his friend, Daniel responded, "After this . . . after the loss of Timmy, after everything, can you honestly say I am?"

Timothy was about to answer, "Yes," but he paused once his mind traveled through the timeline of Daniel and Ayana's life together. From the initial meeting, the ordeal with Satu and Kronte that led to Ayana's coma and Li'l Timothy's birth, when he considered the more recent events, he started to feel that maybe Daniel had a point. Although they shared an envious and almost supernatural kind of love, the two also shared a bond of tragedy that seemed as if Lucifer himself were the architect. However, he couldn't allow himself to fall into Daniel's self-loathing. It was bad enough they lost the most precious thing in their lives, but if they didn't make it as a couple, it would be all for nothing.

"Danny, although you two have been through a shit-load of fucked-up situations, you two are still standing. Although you're not on good terms, you still can fix things. You just have to want to."

"I don't think she wants to."

"What do you mean?"

Daniel looked at his friend and gave him every detail of the night they lost Li'l Timothy and perhaps their love. After he was done, Timothy could feel anger build in his chest that made beads of sweat appear on his nose and forehead. Aggressively breathing while staring at the closed door of the room Ayana was in, Timothy jumped to his feet and stormed over to her room. Daniel tried to stop him, but Timothy snatched away and started banging on the door.

"Ayana, I need to talk to you."

"Timothy, go away. I don't want to speak to you or anyone. Just go away."

Inhaling deeply while closing his eyes, Timothy responded, "I'm not going anywhere until you come out here."

Grunting loudly, Ayana jumped off the bed, ran over to the door, and snatched it open, screaming, "What, Timothy?"

"You fucked John? Tell me you didn't. Please tell me you didn't fuck that murdering muthafucka."

Ayana's eyes moved toward the left until they found Daniel. She sent a heart-chilling stare his way and then responded, "Not that it's any of your business who I may have fucked, but since you two are in such a talkative mood, why don't you ask your friend about the bitch's name he so easily screamed out while she was fucking him like they'd been doing it for months?"

"Ayana, you know damned well the situation with that. You can't hold him responsible for that night. He was doing it to save Timothy."

"Yeah, and where is my son now, Timothy? Where is he? My baby is in . . . He's in a box at some dark and cold funeral home instead of in my arms. So, what was it all for? Huh? He's still dead. My baby is dead."

Ayana began to break down, and Timothy reached out to her and held her in his arms. Ayana buried her face in his chest and cried out in pain. Daniel walked over to her side and reached out for her. Ayana felt him standing next to her, and she looked up at him, surprised to see the look of love in his eyes. She quickly looked away like a frightened child, but Daniel refused to be rejected by her again, so he reached out to her, gently pulled her away from Timothy, and held her in his arms. Initially, she refused to embrace him back, only allowing her arms to dangle by her side, reminiscent of when they first met. Just like before, Daniel allowed his emotional energy to pour into her as he closed his eyes in anticipation of her embrace. His expectation was destroyed, though, when Ayana pulled away, saying, "I can't. I just can't anymore. I'm sorry, Daniel," and walked back into her room and shut the door behind her.

Timothy's mouth hung open as he watched his friend's eyes well with tears. He had no idea things had gotten this bad, and watching Ayana give up on their love was the nail in the coffin in their love story.

Damn.

Chapter Sixteen

Let Me Help You Grieve

One week later
Chicago, Illinois

Timothy walked into the massive church with Simone on his arm, and suddenly, everyone's eyes were on them. Simone's chin slowly lifted as she enjoyed the attention. Timothy's skin crawled at the way their disapproving stares made him feel, having the high-profile, married woman hang on his arm as if they were an item. At the front of the church was the tiny coffin that housed the remains of their little angel, surrounded by massive flower arrangements and pictures of the beautiful toddler smiling, his innocent eyes staring through everyone. When they finally reached the front seating area, Timothy and Simone looked at two possible sitting places. One was next to Daniel's parents, and the other was next to Meagan. Simone smiled like the sun as she led Timothy to the latter of the two choices, perching her amazing ass in the seat next to Meagan.

The spread of her backside covered the space and spilled over until it grazed against Meagan, whose nostrils flared while her skin turned redder by the second. Meagan tried to look ahead, but she couldn't help herself from looking over at the stunning woman and a solemn Timothy, who pretended he didn't notice her stares of shock and anger. Her building jealousy almost made her get up and sit next to Daniel's parents, but she refused to give either of them the satisfaction, so she forced herself through it as the farewell ceremony continued.

The funeral was difficult to sit through, and Ayana's agonizing cries of pain made it even harder. After the burial, Timothy decided it was time to take Simone home before the media had a field day with her accompanying him to the funeral. The last thing he needed was for rumors to grace the ears of her husband and ruin their partnership. As Timothy started driving toward the Eisenhower Expressway, Simone looked around in the front passenger seat confused, tapped him on the shoulder, and asked, "Umm, Tim, where are you going?"

"I'm taking you home. Don't you live in South Barrington?"

"Yes, when my husband is home. That house is entirely too big for me to stay there alone."

"Really?" Timothy responded, looking at her suspiciously. "How big is it?"

"Ninety-eight hundred square feet, not including the lower level."

"Oh shit, that *is* huge."

"Exactly, so when he's away, I usually stay at my penthouse condo near Millennium Park, but tonight, I need you to take me to my townhome in Hyde Park."

"Wait? What? Why do you have a condo downtown and a townhome on the South Side?"

"Because a girl needs privacy, and the condo downtown has too many neighbors and windows."

"Da fuck? What are you and Mr. Karlov doing in that townhouse that you can't do downtown?"

Me and Max ain't doing shit tonight. Tonight's about Tim and Simone. You just don't know it yet, Simone thought as she turned away, smiling to herself, refusing to answer his question. Noticing she wasn't going to continue the conversation, Timothy grinned and headed south on Lake Shore Drive, toward Simone's secret hideaway while thinking . . . *Wait a minute. Why am I taking her to her secret hideaway instead of her downtown condo?*

Half an hour later, Timothy pulled up in front of a large and impressive Greystone townhome with massive, tinted windows covering its frontal exterior. A black wrought iron gate surrounded the front yard and driveway that led to a four-car garage in the rear. Timothy stopped his Mercedes in front of the house, although Simone had reached into her purse and activated the automated gate to let him into the driveway. Looking straight ahead while trying to keep his head clear of any thoughts of what he and Simone could be doing if she invited him inside, Timothy said, "Thank you for accompanying me today. I really didn't want to go alone, and I appreciate you taking time out of your day to go with me."

Smiling, Simone looked at Timothy and responded, "You're more than welcome, Tim."

Nodding, Timothy replied while refusing to look at Simone, who was staring at him like a hungry lioness. "Okay. Good night, Mrs. Karlov."

Giggling, Simone responded while licking her lips, "You think calling me by my marital name will stop me from inviting you inside my townhome and inside of me?"

Trying to calm his growing excitement, he responded, "Basically, especially after leading me on in the elevator at your office. I'm not really in the mood to drive home

with 'Bobby Blue Balls' because you've decided to start
something and not finish it."

"Oh, baby, trust me. I *will* finish you tonight. The
elevator wasn't planned, but after you left the office, I
just had to taste your lips again. I'd forgotten how . . .
mmm . . . blessed you are, and after that reminder, well, I
needed to get you somewhere I can have you all to myself.
No interruptions or prying eyes."

"Oh, so that's what that was?"

Simone started to seductively move closer to Timothy,
pressing her lips against his neck and slowly running
her tongue along his skin. His entire body ignited as he
inhaled and closed his eyes while her tongue sent him
messages words could never express.

"What are you trying to do to me?" he asked while his
body slowly gave in to her.

"Helping you grieve, baby. Let me help you grieve."

A brush of her hand over his groin was the final straw,
and Timothy quickly pulled the car into the driveway.
While he maneuvered the car down the long and narrow
driveway, Simone climbed into his lap, kissing him
passionately. His inhibitions broke free when he felt her
tongue explore his mouth while she grinded on him, and
he closed his eyes, allowing himself to let go. A sudden
loud bang and violent jolt momentarily broke the two
forbidden lovers' concentration as Timothy's car ran into
the side of the garage. Swearing loudly, Timothy hopped
out of his vehicle and ran around to the front to look at
the damage to his hood and headlights.

Simone strolled over to him, grabbed him by his tie,
and said, "Don't worry about that. I'll take care of it.
I'm rich, remember?" She then pulled him behind her,
leading him by his tie through the back door of her townhome. Timothy could barely take in his surroundings as
Simone whisked him past the kitchen, living areas, and

straight into her master bedroom. The room was pitch black, and when she turned on the lights, his eyes beheld a bedroom that seemed designed for a queen. The bed sitting in the middle of the floor was massive and at least four times the size of a California King. It was covered in red and black sheets, which appeared to be made of the most expensive material Timothy had ever seen. Turning to face Timothy, Simone stripped down to nothing and jumped into his arms, wrapping her legs around his waist and whispering, "Make me remember."

Timothy carried her to the edge of the bed and tossed her on it. Simone moaned while she watched Timothy rip off his clothes, and once he was completely naked, she grinned and said, "Wait—let me look at you." Her eyes traveled over his impressively maintained landscape. The dark chocolate of his skin appeared like someone melted a perfect blend of exquisite chocolates all over him.

"Come here. Come stand right here next to me," Simone whispered. As Timothy got closer, she threw her legs over the side of the bed and waited for him to stand in front of her. Her mouth was in a perfect position at this height, and she wanted to submit to him. She got down on her knees and in one smooth gulp, swallowed him whole. Her warm and wet mouth caressed him while her tongue embraced the bottom of his shaft as she gently pulled him out of her mouth and then swallowed him again. Timothy's knees buckled each time he felt himself invade her throat.

Oh my God.

Looking up at the rapture he was experiencing in her mouth turned Simone's center into a leaking dam of desire, and she suddenly wanted to play with herself while she pleased him. When her hand reached her center, her moisture ran over her fingers as she parted her southern lips and began to play one of her favorite songs of ecstasy. The faster her fingers played, the more intense her mouth sang to him, humming and sucking until he could barely stand. Pulling him out of her mouth with a loud pop, Simone got up and sat on the edge of the bed while licking her wet and slimy fingers. Watching her taste her own nectar drove Timothy insane, and he decided he wanted a drink from her fountain as well. Throwing her legs up and over his shoulders, he opened his mouth and feasted on her. He'd been starving for her taste for years, and he made it perfectly clear just how hungry his desire was as his mouth brought her to climax in less than a minute.

Trembling and trying to push his head away, Simone screamed as she felt him fight against her while he continued to lap and suck on her clitoris with his full lips and tongue. Feeling the explosion building up inside of her again, Simone reached down with her nails and ran them up his back, slightly cutting his dark skin. Cringing in pain, Timothy pulled back, grabbed her by the hips, and entered her in one sudden thrust. Her screams of pleasure increased his excitement as he fucked her with long, deep, and forceful thrusts that made her expensive bed shake as if it were made at a flea market. As Timothy dug deeper into her, he couldn't recall a woman that was wetter, tighter, or more sensational.

The two of them ravaged each other well into the next morning. Around 1:00 p.m., after taking a hot shower, Timothy crept out of her townhome, leaving her sprawled out over the side of her bed, sleeping as if in a coma.

Fuck. What did I just get myself into?

Chapter Seventeen

The Purple Room

Several weeks later, Timothy sat behind his new office desk in the northern Chicago suburb of Elk Grove Village while Simone rode him in his high-back leather chair. She loved fucking with all the lights on, and even in broad daylight, she still made Timothy turn on all the lights, even his desk lamp. No matter how many times he was inside of her, it always felt like the first time—and the first time was fantastic. Timothy began to grip her ass, and his mouth opened wider as he felt himself getting closer with each turn of her hips. Suddenly, the booming sound of Maximillian Karlov's voice filled the hallway right outside his office door.

"Where is he? Where is that son of a bitch?"

They could hear Timothy's secretary stuttering as she tried to answer the intimidating billionaire. Simone quickly jumped off Timothy's lap and crawled under his desk. Her mouth began to water as she looked at Timothy's hardness, throbbing and dripping with her juices.

Mmm . . .

She wanted to swallow him, but she knew that her jealous husband would discover them if she did. Simone kept her eyes closed and tried to think of something else besides the large, ten-incher in front of her. Without warning, Timothy's office door flung open, and Maximillian stormed in, yelling, "Doctor Avers, you son of a bitch. You lucky son of a bitch."

Timothy's face erupted in confusion because he was sure the billionaire had found out their affair until he noticed the piece of paper in his hand. Mr. Karlov kept waving it around like a flag of victory, and soon, the realization of what that document meant hit Timothy, and his face lit up like a summer day after a storm.

"Is that what I think it is?"

"Yes, it is. The FDA not only approved your vaccine, but they are also holding a huge dinner in your honor. So, I hope you have your best suits pressed and ironed because you're gonna be the most famous doctor in history."

Simone's eyes shot open when she heard the news and without thinking, she swallowed Timothy down like a Tootsie Roll. His ass lifted up in the seat as he tried to hold in the loud, "Oh shit," that was dancing around on his tongue. Mr. Karlov's head tilted to the right as he watched Timothy's reaction, and his eyelids and brows slowly lowered.

"What the hell is wrong with you, Doctor? I just told you your vaccine has been green-lighted for production and distribution, and all you could do is wiggle in your fucking chair?"

Simone suddenly deepthroated him, while making wavelike motions with her tongue, causing Timothy's body to tremble.

"I'm sorry, Mr. Karl . . . lululu . . . lov . . . it'sssss . . . been a long day," Timothy stammered while gripping the arms of his chair as if his life depended on it.

"What the fuck are you talking about? It's only ten in the morning."

"I mean, it's been a long morning. Yeah, a long morning."

"Hmmm, a long morning, huh? Something isn't right in here, and I'm going to get to the bottom of it."

Suddenly, the suspicious billionaire's eyes started looking over Timothy's office, trying to find anything out of place. He knew something wasn't right because the doctor was still sitting in his chair and looking like he was about to pass out. As his eyes looked over toward the sitting area to his right, he noticed a woman's purse on the black leather couch, and it didn't take long for him to recognize the design. His nostrils immediately flared, and his heart rate increased as his eyes turned toward Timothy, red with rage. Mr. Karlov was not a man who wasted time, so he wasn't going to ask the doctor whose purse was lying on his couch. No need to ask a question that would undoubtedly receive a lie as a response.

"What was my wife doing here?"

Timothy's eyes that were half-open and fluttering from the oral assault he was receiving under his desk immediately shot wide open.

"Your wife, Mrs. Karlov?"

"I only have one wife, Doctor Avers. Is my wife in this building? Is she in this office with you, under your desk hiding while hiding, your dick in her mouth?"

"Hey, Mr. Karlov, you are out of line."

"You still haven't answered my question, Doctor."

Suddenly, Simone's mouth closed around Timothy's shaft as she began to increase her speed and suction, refusing to allow him out of her mouth. Timothy inhaled deeply as he attempted to control his need to yell out in pleasure. He then looked the angry husband in the eyes and said, "Yes, your wife *was* here, but that was a couple of days ago. She came here to check up on our progress. She got a call from you, I believe, that seemed like an emergency, and she ran out of here, leaving her purse behind."

Mr. Karlov's already large and intimidating frame seemed to swell with anger with each lie that came out of Timothy's mouth until his skin was strawberry red, and he was balancing his almost 300-pound frame on his tiptoes.

"You must take me for some kind of fool, Doctor. If your story is true, my wife's car keys would not be in that purse."

"She may have caught a cab."

"That's where you're wrong, Doctor. My wife suffers from an acute fear of taxis and taxi drivers, so much so, she needed years of therapy. So, if she ran out of your office a few days ago and forgot her keys, she would've come back, grabbed her purse, and left. Now I could walk over there and check her purse, but I think it's better if I just looked under your desk and save myself the time and trouble."

Maximillian then started walking toward Timothy, and just when he was about to panic, Timothy had an epiphany.

Tell the truth.

"Wait, Mr. Karlov. Stop. There *is* someone under here."

"I knew it. That cheating whore."

"But . . . but . . . It's not your wife. I needed to release some tension, and since I don't have the time for mean-ingful connections, I called . . . a . . . well, you know."

Well, a half-truth.

Mr. Karlov suddenly stopped walking, turned his head slightly to the left, and asked, "A prostitute?"

"Well, I wouldn't call her that."

"A whore?"

"Well, um . . ."

"Then who the fuck is she, Doctor? Is she a whore—or is she my wife? Say it," Maximillian yelled while he started to move toward the desk again.

"A whore. Yes. She's a fucking ho bitch. A nasty, dick-sucking, paid-to-play, ho bitch."

Simone scraped her teeth along Timothy's shaft, almost making him scream out in soprano from the pain.

Add something else to that "ho bitch," and I'll bite this shit off, Simone thought, as she continued to suck him.

Mr. Karlov paused for a second and appeared to be tuning his ear in preparation of a sound he was anticipating. But after a few seconds, he began to smile and back away from Timothy's desk. Laughing gingerly, Maximillian sighed as if the weight of the world had been lifted off his chest, and suddenly, he appeared to be apologetic. Timothy looked at him as if he were insane, and once the billionaire noticed his reaction, he said, "My wife *really* hates being called a whore, even worse, a ho bitch. It's to the point she will get pretty irate or violent if you do. So, if she were under there sucking you off, and we called her those terrible names, she wouldn't hesitate to defend herself. I'm sorry if I made your . . . ahem . . . *company* feel uncomfortable. I'll leave the approval document over here and take my wife's purse with me. I would hate for her to have to come all the way here just to get it. I'm sure you understand."

"Oh, sure. Be my guest and no problem. I know how it looks, but thanks for understanding."

"You're welcome, Doctor. Now, tell your 'companion' to hurry up so that you can get back to work. We have the world to save and billions to make. Have a great day, Doctor."

Then as suddenly as he appeared, Mr. Karlov was gone, carrying his wife's purse in his arms like a small pet. As soon as Maximillian closed the door behind him, Timothy erupted inside Simone's mouth, and she took all that he gave her down her throat like a champ. Collapsing on top of his desk, Timothy began to hyperventilate while he tried to scold Simone for almost getting them caught—or worse. Climbing from under his desk, Simone wiped the sides of her mouth and said, "You almost got your dick bit off with all that extra shit you added. Calling me that name was bad enough. If I didn't love sucking your cock more than I hate being called a ho bitch, we would all be in deep shit."

"I can't . . . I can't believe you did that while he was standing a few feet from you."

"If a married woman can fuck you in private, she should be able to fuck you in public as well. Even with her husband in the next room, watching the game with his friends and family."

"Huh? What kind of philosophy is that?"

"The philosophy of an adulterous woman. Look, I know what kind of woman I am, and I embrace it. I'm not like all these other women who fuck around on their spouses yet pretend they have morals or standards. Fuck that. I'm a cheater, that's who I am, and I love it. Haven't done it in a while . . . almost five years now. But I'm always looking for my next side dish, and you, by far, are my favorite meal."

"Simone, this is fucking crazy. Do you know what your husband would do if he caught us? What that could do to this vaccine?"

"Stop tripping, Timothy. You have an ironclad agreement. He could've caught your dick in my ass, and he still couldn't back out of this deal, so relax. I will say I was definitely impressed by how you used the phone call the other day to explain why my purse was here, even though we were at my condo at the time. It was so fucking sexy to be riding your face while I talked to him on the phone. And let's not pretend you didn't show out while I was on the phone with him either. You went all in, trying to rush me off the phone with him."

"I have no idea what you're talking about," he responded with a mischievous grin.

"Yeah, sure, you don't. Now, if you don't mind, I need a ride home."

"Wait. What the fuck? Are your keys really in that purse he just took?"

"Yep, so let's pray he doesn't look inside before I get home."

Fuck my life.

An hour later, Timothy pulled into the garage of Simone's Hyde Park townhouse, feeling conflicted about the three-week affair he'd been having with her. Like an old fool, he believed their relationship was built on romance, that their old love was being rekindled. However, after her "pro-cheater" proclamation, he understood he was nothing to her but an old toy refurbished and sparkling for her to play with.

"Are you coming in?" Simone asked while appearing impatient in the front passenger seat.

"Huh, woman, are you crazy? What you *should* be doing is rushing home to grab that purse before he looks inside."

"Pssht . . . Please, I'm not worried about Max. He's a creature of habit and believes his money keeps me loyal. He's too arrogant and selfish to want to find out if his pussy is wayward out here in these streets."

Shaking his head, Timothy whispered, "Unbelievable."

"What'd you say?"

"Nothing, Simone. I'd love to come in, but I have a lot of work to do."

"Yes, you do. Just thinking about all that money is making my pussy squishy and hot."

The thought of her "squishy and hot" made Timothy's knees jerk roll, but he decided it was best if he left immediately, before he found himself too far gone to see her for what she was.

"So that's a no?"

Sighing, Timothy responded, "Yeah, I'm afraid so."

"Okay, cool, but do you think you can carry that box over there to my basement?" Simone asked, pointing to a large box standing in the corner of her garage.

"Sure, what is it?"

"It's just some linen I had shipped from Italy a few months ago. So, it's not that heavy."

"Linens? And you couldn't do it yourself or get someone else to carry it down to your basement?" Timothy asked while giving her the side eye.

"Tim, who would I call to carry that in this place? And look at the size of that thing."

Looking at the size of the box and reminding himself of the secret nature of her townhome, Timothy nodded and got out of the car. As soon as he tried wrapping his arms around the box, he discovered Simone wasn't lying. The box wasn't heavy, but its size made it difficult to grasp. His anxiety subsided as he lifted it on his shoulders and walked behind Simone. Once inside, following her to the door leading down to the basement, Timothy noticed the basement door was locked, and the look of confusion on his face made Simone smile as she led him downstairs. Halfway down the stairs, the smell of lavender filled his nose, its relaxing effect taking hold immediately. Once he got to the bottom of the stairs, he looked around in the dark and asked, "Turn on the lights, please."

"Oh, baby, you don't have to ask *me* twice," Simone seductively responded, right before the entire basement lit up, and what came into focus made his mouth and the box fall to the floor. Timothy found himself surrounded by walls covered in purple-colored velvet and floors covered in a darker shade of plush purple carpet. In the middle of the room were several S&M contraptions that appeared as if they dropped straight out of the most sexually depraved minds alive. Numerous types of whips, paddles, chains, and other scream-inducing gadgets also hung from the purple walls. While Timothy looked around him like a sheep trapped in a lion's den, on the far side of the room, Simone playfully rocked on a swing made of purple leather that hung from the black-colored ceiling.

"What the *en-tire* fuck?" Timothy gasped as he slowly backed out of the room.

"Welcome to my royal chamber. Come, bow to your queen."

"Ha . . . yeah, riiiight. Not gonna happen," he said and started to walk up the stairs.

"You mean to tell me you're not curious about what I'll let you do to me *if* you come play with me? I haven't even begun to show you just how much fun I can be, but if you come down here and play . . . mmm, baby, I will show you so much more."

Her sultry voice and the prospect of experiencing another level of sexual bliss with her mesmerized him, and he hesitated, and that's all Simone needed to convince him to stay for a while and play.

"Come here and bow to your queen . . . *now*," Simone demanded while pointing to the floor directly in front of her. Timothy looked at her, refusing to move from the stairs leading up and out of her purple torture palace. He looked up the stairs and then back at her. Swallowing hard, he slowly made his way to her. Once he was standing in front of her, Simone got up from the swing and stood in front of him, pointed to the ground, and said, "Kneel."

Timothy looked in her eyes and slowly got down on his knees.

"That's a good boy. Now . . . lower. Bow to me."

"Man, fuck this—"

Simone suddenly placed her leg over his shoulder while pressing her pelvis against his face. Timothy immediately started to grope her ass while trying to bite through her dress and panties. Simone forcefully pushed his head away and said, "Kneel—or we're done."

Timothy's arousal and addiction to her compelled him to bow slowly to her like a loyal subject. Simone lifted her foot and placed her heel on his back. Leaning down until the sharp end began to dig into his flesh, Simone moaned while she looked down at Timothy, bowing to her. He started to move, and she snapped, "Don't you move one fucking inch. If you can't take a little pain, you can't take a little pussy."

Grimacing in pain, Timothy stopped moving as Simone continued to lean more weight on his back. The pain of the heel was becoming unbearable, and just when he couldn't take any more, Simone stood straight up and walked over to a black table in the middle of the room. Looking at Timothy, she ordered him to crawl to her. Moving along the floor on all fours, Timothy crawled to the edge of the table, waiting for her next degrading command.

"That's a good boy. Now rise to your feet, you fucking mutt."

Timothy shook his head and stood up. Simone pushed her body onto his and violently kissed his lips while gyrating against him. Her aggression aroused him, and he quickly forgot the degrading journey he just took on the floor. Timothy started to squeeze her ass, and she suddenly backed away and seductively sat on the edge of the black table. Timothy started to join her, and she quickly placed her foot on his chest, preventing him from coming closer. Breathing forcefully, Timothy backed away while gesturing toward the massive bulge in his pants. Simone looked down at his hard-on and shrugged.

"What the fuck you want me to do about it?"

"I want you to swallow it with your mouth and pussy— *that's* what I want you to do about it."

"What if I say no?"

"Then why are you fucking playing games? I bowed to you, crawled like a fucking dog, and now you're still not done with the games?"

"No, baby, we're just beginning to play."

"I don't have time for this shit. I'm outta here," he said right before he started to walk away from the table.

"If you leave, I will tell my husband about us."

"You wouldn't fucking dare. You would lose everything, maybe even your life."

"Oh, trust me, baby, what I would lose would be child's play compared to your losses. I'm a woman that always has a backup plan, but are you *that* kind of man, Tim?"

Timothy stopped walking and suddenly rushed toward the table. Simone watched him storming toward her, smiled, and scooted farther on top of the table. Once Timothy was in front of her, he grabbed her by her neck and yelled, "I don't have time for your fucking games. I should've never got involved with you, but I will *not* be used by you or anyone else. I am my own man. I control my actions and the outcome—not you or your buffoon of a husband."

Closing her eyes and leaning her head back, Simone whispered, "Choke me harder, baby."

Confusion spread over Timothy's face like a tidal wave as he tried to comprehend what Simone just asked him to do.

"Da fuck you just ask me?"

"You heard me the first time. Do it, or should I get someone else to do it?"

The very thought of another man taking his place in her bed, between her thighs, feeling her wondrous mouth pleasure them to the edge of madness caused a wave of anger and distress to swell inside of him he'd never felt before. Before he could understand his reaction, Timothy was applying pressure around her neck, and Simone responded by undoing his pants and pulling them down with her feet.

"Harder," she gasped as she lay back on the table, allowing Timothy to join her. Reaching down through the peek hole of his boxer briefs, Simone pulled out his manhood, spread her legs, and placed him inside of her.

"Now fuck me like you hate me," she whispered in his ear, and Timothy didn't hesitate to give her exactly what she asked for. His usually deep and sensual strokes transformed into animalistic thrusts of anger while he grunted and continued to apply more pressure around Simone's neck. Her dark skin started to turn purple as her oxygen-deprived body began to protest, and her consciousness began to fade. She could feel herself dying, but the building volcanic eruption that was traveling throughout her body was too priceless to pass up. Timothy was now drowning in his lustful anger, and he didn't notice her eyes fluttering or her hands slapping the top of the table as her body struggled against the oncoming darkness of death.

The longer he ravaged her, the closer he could feel his own climax building, which was growing more intense with each passing second, and all he wanted was to explode inside of her.

"Oh my God!" Trembling while yelling out in pleasure, Timothy felt himself release, and the massive amount of pleasure his body experienced was more than he'd ever felt in his life—more than he could've ever imagined. Suddenly, Simone's body went limp, and Timothy's satisfaction was short-lived as he looked down at her laid out on the table, motionless. Her eyes were wide open and appeared to have lost the light in them, the same light of life and seduction that drew him to her all those years ago.

"Simone?"

His already-accelerated heartbeat went into overdrive as he frantically listened and searched for a pulse or any signs that she was still alive.

Nothing.

Timothy immediately started to give her CPR, and after each cycle that she didn't come to, a sudden feeling of dread came over him as he repeatedly tried to revive her. Leaning in for the sixth time to force air into her limp body, Timothy covered her mouth with his own and forcefully blew down her throat. As he pulled up, he felt her tongue invade his mouth, and her arms wrap around his neck. Shocked, Timothy snatched away from her embrace and looked down at her as she started to tremble from her own near-death orgasmic experience. Scrutinizing her, he noticed the flow of liquid that streamed out of her center like a river. Before he could open his mouth, Simone whispered, "I've never come that hard in my life. Oh my God, Timothy, you are unbelievable."

"Unbelievable? I thought I'd killed you."

"I believe you did, but you also resurrected me. Mmm .. . Baby, let's do that again."

"Oh no, that's enough roughhousing for one day. I'm out. I don't care who you tell at this point."

"Please don't leave. Okay, we don't have to play so hard, but I still want to play, and judging by how hard you came inside of me, you want to keep playing too."

Timothy looked down at Simone, and when she noticed the alarm in his eyes, she sat up and kissed him while stroking his still throbbing muscle.

"Mmm . . . You're still hard for me, baby? Let's not waste it. Come here and feed it to me," she whispered while lying on her back and leading him into her mouth. If there were ever some kryptonite for Timothy's genius and mental strength, it was definitely Simone. As soon as he felt her work him down her throat, all sensible thinking vanished. Within half an hour of being pleased by Simone's mouth, Timothy was willing to do any and everything she asked, and despite his fear of being dominated by her, he soon found out Simone got off on being the dominatrix. She would drive him near insanity with her sexual and mental manipulation and then encourage him to bond and whip her into submission. Timothy tried to pretend he didn't enjoy the experience, watching her dark skin whipped and spanked as he tied her into torturous positions and then fuck her like a stranger. The more unnerving the act, the more she enjoyed it, and he found himself dedicated to bringing her whatever pleasures she desired. Although he was the one inflicting the pain, she was always in control, and by the end of the night, his dedication to her was bordering on insanity. As he drove off into the evening, Timothy reflected on the depraved acts of the evening and smiled.

I fucking love that woman.

Chapter Eighteen

Father Is Highly Disappointed

Three weeks later
Undisclosed location in the Baltic Region

The cobblestone-paved streets and ancient architecture seemed to whisk John away to a time of monarchs and revolutions as he strolled down the market street. A merchant called out to the assassin, offering a deal for some of his edible wares, but John just smiled and waved him off. The mist of his breath seemed to almost freeze in midair, and John quietly cursed as he considered his limited options of places to hide. It was always cold. Even in the summer, the sun seemed weak and powerless to penetrate the cloudy and cold atmosphere of this small yet historic country. He'd crossed the most dangerous group of people the world has ever known, and he was reduced to living in an icebox of a country, just to prolong the inevitable.

The many smells and noises of the open market surrounded him as he maneuvered through the crowded street toward his favorite coffee shop. Suddenly, the cell phone in his pocket began to vibrate, and he stopped walking and closed his eyes, waiting for the end. After a few seconds, he realized no sniper's bullet was coming, so he opened his eyes. With his eyes open, he frowned at the person suddenly invading his personal space in front of him, their presence making him wish for the bullet instead of their unwelcomed face. The vibrant blue hue of their eyes, paired with the unique skin tone, seemed to make their eyes sparkle in the dimming light of the afternoon, and John suddenly realized what all the fuss was about.

"John?"

"Cloe?"

"How did you find me?" he asked while surveying his surroundings.

Tilting her head to the right while smirking, Cloe responded, "Really? You have to ask that question?"

"Right. Very well. Well played, Cloe, well played. At first, I had my suspicions that you were a Trojan horse planted by Father until the night you were supposedly killed."

"You can stroke my ego and private parts later, John. Right now, I have a message from Father that he wanted to be delivered to you personally."

"And what might that message be?"

"Not here. Meet me by the river in two hours."

"Very well. Two hours it is."

Cloe looked the assassin up and down and rolled her eyes, and then she turned to leave. She suddenly stopped and said while raising her index finger in the air, "Oh, and, John, please don't embarrass yourself and not show up. I'd hate to put a bullet in you before I deliver Father's message."

Giving her a sarcastic grin, he responded, "I wouldn't dream of it, dearie."

Cloe then disappeared in the crowded market as quickly as she appeared. Exhaling, John slowly pulled out his cell phone and looked at the missed call scrolled across the screen. Instead of a phone number, a sequence of numbers and letters rolled across the screen, the same type of code he would get when a new contract was assigned. The idea of Father giving him another contract after his betrayal sent a cold chill through him, even colder than the frigid winds that licked at his exposed face and hands. Knowing in a couple of hours he could be taking his last breath, John decided to continue his journey to the coffee shop and have a final cup of their delicious brew before curtain call.

Two hours later, John stood along the riverbanks with his hands exposed and his back to the water. The tranquil sound of the flowing winter river calmed his nerves as he silently stood while making peace with his actions leading him to this point. He wanted to see his death coming, and as expected, Cloe appeared out of the brush with her gun aimed at him. John was genuinely impressed by the way she moved without alerting him of her presence.

Very impressive.

She slowly moved closer to him, pressed her gun's muzzle in the middle of his forehead, and coldly stared into his eyes. John stared back at her, unbothered by the impending bullet that could tear through his skull at any moment. Cloe was equally impressed by John's steel resolve, even in the face of death. Smiling, she took a few steps back while keeping her weapon aimed at John, and said, "I'm not here to kill you."

"Excuse me?"

"You heard me. Father is extremely disappointed in you, but he believes you are the best. I would argue that sentiment, but your record is undeniable. So, he's offering you a chance to redeem yourself by completing one last harvest."

"One last harvest? I thought this was redemption?"

"It is, but Father isn't stupid enough to believe your loyalty is unwavering. You allowed your feelings for another man's wife to get in the way of your dedication. So, Father has decided to allow you to redeem yourself so that you can live out the rest of your life without worrying when someone like me will suddenly end it."

"Fine, I'll bite."

"Don't be so quick to accept this contract, Mr. Smith. Some particulars will make things very difficult for you. I know you've tried to break the code on your phone and found you were unable to review the details, correct?"

"Yeah, so?"

"Well, let me send you the encryption's translation so that you can look at the details and decide if death is better than what Father is asking of you."

Cloe then used her free hand to reach into her pocket and send the code to John's phone. His phone immediately began to vibrate in the breast pocket of his coat, and he slowly started to reach for it. Cloe took a few steps back and warned, "Very slowly, John. Don't make me get nervous. It's already colder than a witch's nipple out here. One false jerk and pop goes your melon."

John slowed down his motion until he could pull his phone out without his "melon going pop." After a few button presses, the encryption software began to work, and the picture that scrolled over his screen made the usually calm assassin gasp, the frigid air drying his throat instantly. The ramifications of the harvest would ruin whatever dream he may have of finding some type of normalcy in life, but he was still confused. He looked up at Cloe with a burning question he'd been dying to ask since she showed up in the market.

"Why would you kill the baby? What was the purpose?"

"The Bennett boy still lives. He's my assurance that you will complete your harvest as Father commands if you choose to accept it."

"So, once I complete this harvest, the boy will be returned to his mother?"

"I didn't say that. But he will be allowed to live once we both complete our harvests."

Interesting, John thought as he began to calculate and piece together the numerous factors of what harvest Cloe could possibly be on and how Ayana's son could be an intricate part of her plans.

"Do you know what you're asking me to do?"

"I'm not asking you to do anything. Father is giving you a choice. If it were up to me, I would've killed you the moment you killed my prodigy at the Bennetts' mansion. I'd been training him for over three years, and you ended all that hard work in less than ten seconds. If it weren't for Father's strict orders to give you this choice, I would end this right here and now."

That was a wasted three years of training, John thought while trying hard not to smile.

"So, he was *your* assistant? No wonder he had his back to the door, a major no-no in our line of work. But I'm confused about why would you go to such lengths? You could've killed them all at any moment. Why the theatrics?"

"A girl has needs, John, and that doctor is a fine specimen. I wanted to experience him before I killed him, but you . . . You ruined everything. I lost the contract, my partner, and the money because of you. I should kill you right now."

Ignoring her anger toward him, John responded amusedly, "So you decided to take a little something for yourself before killing the good doctor? I don't know if that's sick or brilliant. I'm conflicted. So, you two never—"

"Not before that night, no. I know he was tempted, but he never fell for any of my advances, and I'd gotten pretty bold before that night."

Interesting.

"Wait a minute. Something isn't adding up here. The way you two were together, the connection, the emotion, that fucking scream that came out of his mouth. I heard it all the way downstairs in that massive eyesore they called home. How did you get the man to even respond to you in that way?"

Shrugging, Cloe responded, "I might've cheated a little."

"Wait. Come again? How did you . . . cheat?"

"I may have used a nerve enhancer cream when I started to stroke his—"

"No need to go into details. I get it."

"I was supposed to be his last piece of pussy, so I wanted him to *really* fucking enjoy it."

"Wow . . . just wow. You know, with all the evil I've done on this entire planet, I am the last person to judge anyone. But something inside is still obliging me to say this to you . . . You ain't shit."

"Yeah, you aren't one to judge, especially since you lied to her husband about fucking his wife. At least, I actually fucked *my* mark. You just imagined you fucked yours. As if a woman like that would have a man like you."

"Okay, so back to your threats. You can't kill me unless I refuse this contract. So, if I decide to forego this harvest, and I die here today, who gets this harvest?"

Cloe responded with a smile so evil it disturbed John to his core. He wasn't afraid to die. He'd killed so many people that he felt it was only right that Karma came to collect her debt. But he knew the woman in front of him would complete not only this harvest but also the previous harvest he ruined. John could tell from her psychotic smile that Cloe would do anything to get revenge, and she was planning to go against the wishes of Father and kill him once his harvest was complete. As much as he was prepared to lay his burdens by the riverside, he had no other choice but to take the contract. He hoped Ayana would one day understand why he decided to say yes to such a mission. He never thought it would be possible, but somehow, Ayana got to him. Although he lied to her husband when he implied he and Ayana had physical dealings, he'd fantasized since he left South Sudan of all the possibilities.

Cloe studied the assassin with eager anticipation of him declining the harvest and the prospect of finally having her revenge. She knew he wasn't afraid to die, but to carry out this latest request would put more than his life in jeopardy. Steadying her breathing, she readied herself to feel the satisfaction of ending the life of the man who always stood in her way of being the best. Looking up from his phone and then looking directly at Cloe, John said calmly, "I accept the harvest."

The look of disappointment and anger that exploded on her face almost made what he would lose worth it—almost.

"Assassin, I will tell you this one time. I am not Father. I don't forgive or give second chances. If you get in my way, I *will* kill you."

Yeah, right, as if you could.

Chapter Nineteen

Janus

Three months later
Chicago, Illinois

Timothy watched Daniel sprawled out on the couch like a crackhead needing a fix. He'd lost everything but his money, but the way he was spending it, Timothy feared he would lose that as well. Ayana went back to South Sudan to continue her campaign a few weeks after the funeral without a goodbye or giving her husband a clue if their marriage were still salvageable or officially over. Timothy figured she needed to fill up her grief with something meaningful. Otherwise, she would also go insane like the semiconscious man in front of him.

As he watched his friend grovel in drunken guilt, Timothy felt like the worst friend in the world because he hadn't seen Daniel in over six weeks. He tried to excuse his lack of support for his best friend due to his obligation of getting the vaccine out to the public. However, the truth was he'd been either spending every free second he could between Simone's legs or thinking about the next time he would be allowed inside the "Purple Palace."

Now, standing in Daniel's nasty living room while Daniel drooled and groaned from extreme intoxication, he couldn't make any more excuses.

I'm the shittiest friend in the world.

"Danny, listen. I came over here because I want you to come to my awards dinner that the president is holding in my honor."

Daniel's eyes rolled in his head as he growled at his friend like a stray dog. Timothy walked over and flopped down on the couch next to him, then poured himself a drink. Leaning back, Timothy turned toward his friend and said, "Listen, Danny, I know life has dealt you a fucked-up hand. But you're stronger than this. You can't give up. I know my godson wouldn't want to see you like this."

Daniel turned and looked at Timothy and chuckled while taking another long pull from his bottle of cheap liquor. Timothy noticed the bottle of four-dollar alcohol and snatched it out of his hand.

"Dude, what the fuck? You're worth millions. If you're gonna drink yourself to death, at least do it with a better brand of liquor than this ghetto ratchet shit."

"Fuck you very much for your diagnosis, Doctor. Now, give me back my bottle."

"Oh, he speaks. I thought my best friend had allowed the liquor to pickle his brain until he's Dr. Frankenstein's monster."

"Timmy, why are you here?"

"Didn't you just hear me ask you to come to my award dinner?"

"Yeah, I did, but you could've texted me or emailed the invitation. Why are you really here?"

"I miss my friend, that's all."

"Bullshit. You feel guilty for abandoning your friend—twice."

"Danny—"

"No, it's cool. I know you're out there saving the world, one unfaithful wife at a time, and you don't have time for your friends and family anymore. I hope that pussy is a better fuck than you are a bullshitter."

"Oh gawd, yes, it is," Timothy responded eagerly and then caught himself when he noticed Daniel staring at him as if he were a fool. Sucking his teeth, Daniel shook his head as he got up from the couch and stumbled across the living room.

"Timothy, I can't believe that you would get involved with that woman, knowing she's married."

"Wait. Are you judging me? *You?* After you and Cloe, you're gonna stand there and judge me?"

"I told you before; I didn't sleep with her before that night."

"Really? And who would believe you after your reaction to her?"

Shaking his head and looking even more defeated, Daniel responded, "No one."

"Exactly, so don't bring Simone into this. We all have our devices and imperfections. I came here to invite you to one of the biggest nights of my life. I want my best friend there, and I don't want any excuses about why you can't make it. You better get yourself together and get your ass to that awards dinner."

Timothy then stood up and stormed out of Daniel's condo. The loud bang of his door closing seemed to jolt Daniel out of the purgatory of intoxication, and he collapsed on the floor in a pile of flesh, tears, and anguish while repeating his son's name.

Three nights later, the entire city of Chicago was buzzing with the news that one of its very own sons had discovered a cure for cancer. With the president of the United States and numerous other heads of state from around the world in attendance, traffic was impossible, and that's why Timothy decided to charter a helicopter to take him to his event. Sitting in the luxury helicopter as it flew over downtown Chicago was an exhilarating experience. He felt a surge of energy flow through him as he looked down on the citywide gridlock and felt untouchable. He was flying solo because Maximillian was escorting Simone to the event. The very thought of him touching her caused beads of sweat to appear on the back of Timothy's neck and the tip of his nose.

As the helicopter started to land on top of the Hilton Chicago, Timothy tried his best to relax. The last thing he wanted to do was ruin his night by being jealous of Maximillian's access to his own wife. He thought he knew what he was getting himself into, but as the helipad attendant opened the helicopter's door, Timothy realized he was in over his head.

The hotel staff treated him like royalty as they flanked him inside the hotel and escorted him to the penthouse suite, where someone would interview before he headed down to the ball. The staff accompanied him to the door of his suite, and once they were sure he was safely inside, they all left to go about their duties for the big evening.

As soon as Timothy walked into the suite, his nose caught a familiar scent that immediately sent him into panic mode because of the impossibility of her being here, and he quickly turned to run out the door. Unfortunately, the clicking sound of the safety of her handgun being removed made him freeze.

"Doctor Avers, why don't you join us?"

"Us?"

Outside the hotel, draped in the most elegant green and gold traditional African dress that was both free-flowing and elegant, Ayana stepped out of the limo alongside

Patrick. They walked down the red carpet toward the hotel entrance, waving at the cameras and smiling. Since Timothy's death, Ayana hated Chicago, and the memories of her dramatic experiences came back as soon as their plane landed. It was a beautiful summer's night, but her delicate chocolate skin was covered in goose bumps, terrified to run into Daniel during this event, and the emotional trauma it would cause her. She initially declined to attend, but Patrick insisted on them going, saying she was too close to the situation not to attend. Patrick noticed her eyes searching the crowd, and he leaned closer to her ear and whispered, "I doubt he'll be here tonight. My sources have told me that he hasn't been himself since Timothy's death."

Nodding, Ayana moved her ear away from his mouth, annoyed by the fact he sent her down memory lane at a moment as public as this, knowing the very mention of Timothy's name brought a flood of tears out of her, no matter where she was. Swallowing hard and stretching her eyes open to try to hold back the tears, Ayana started walking ahead of Patrick to avoid him saying anything else.

After nearly an hour of short interviews, meet and greets with other world leaders, and a countless number of pictures taken, Patrick and Ayana sat down at their assigned table in the grand ballroom. The beautifully decorated ballroom should've taken Ayana's breath away, but these days, she didn't have the stomach to appreciate anything beautiful.

Without warning, the president of Nigeria appeared out of nowhere and leaned down to greet Ayana warmly.

"Mrs. Bennett, we are so excited to see you here. I would also like to extend my deepest condolences concerning the loss of your son."

Fighting back the tears, Ayana nodded and said, "Thank you, Mr. President. I appreciate it."

"It's my pleasure. Will your husband, Doctor Bennett, be in attendance tonight? My wife and I would like to get our books signed by him."

That's it.

Ayana abruptly got up from the table and left the ballroom in a hurry. Outside the ballroom's entrance, she asked one of the porters to show her the direction of the ladies' room. Given the directions, Ayana quickly made her way to the restroom to drain out all the poison from her emotional wounds that everyone kept reopening. As she started to walk through the bathroom door, a voice from behind her whispered, "Come with me, Mrs. Bennett. If you try anything, I will dig this knife into your liver. Do you understand?"

Terrified, Ayana nodded as she felt the sharp end of the blade poke through her dress.

"Now, move toward the elevators."

Ayana started walking while trying to turn her head, and the increased pressure of the knife being pushed harder into her flesh warned her to keep looking forward. As soon as they walked into the elevator, her kidnapper instructed her to press the penthouse button.

"I thought you died with my son."

Cloe smiled and responded, "Well, you thought wrong. Just like you thought your husband and I were having an affair."

"What?" Ayana yelled and aggressively bolted toward Cloe.

"Back up, bitch, before I ruin that beautiful dress," Cloe warned while pointing her eight-inch army knife in Ayana's direction. Backing up, Ayana put her back against the elevator wall and said, "You made me believe my husband was unfaithful to me? Why?"

"'Cause you were stupid enough to think he would cheat on you. Look at yourself. What man in his right mind would actually fuck another bitch over you? He might be tempted, but honestly, he would have to be damn near retarded to take that chance. And let's face it, your husband isn't that stupid with his sexy and big, sweet, dick ass," Cloe responded while licking her lips.

"Fuck you!"

"No, bitch, *I* made your man eat my pussy while you watched. *I* fucked your man and made you watch. *I* made your man scream *my* name while you watched. *I* made you fall out of love with him and turn your back on everything you two built together. Then *I* took your precious little boy from you—right under your nose. No, you stupid bitch. I fucked *you*."

"So, you're the one responsible for my baby's death?"

"Actually, your little Timmy is still alive and well, but he has a new mommy now."

Fuck it.

Ayana leaped forward, leading with a straight right that Cloe quickly sidestepped, but she didn't see the left uppercut. Ayana connected her punch, sending Cloe in the air and the knife flying out of her hand. Ayana watched the knife soar through the air and anticipated where it would start to descend so that she could snatch it out of the air. Falling on the floor on her ass, Cloe noticed what Ayana intended to do, and she jumped up from the floor, ramming her body into Ayana's midsection like a linebacker. Ayana's back slammed into the elevator's wall and metal hand railing, causing intense pain to burn through her back. She watched the knife fall to the floor, and Cloe turned at the sound of its metal blade sliding across the marble floor in the elevator. Ayana quickly lifted her elbow and brought it down on the back of Cloe's neck, sending her to the floor.

With Cloe's grip around her waist loosened, Ayana dove toward the knife. Ignoring the pain in her neck, Cloe reached out and grabbed Ayana's ankles while she was in midflight and swung her like a bat toward the wall to her left. Ayana's body hit the wall with a loud thud and fell to the floor. Cloe, seeing an opportunity, reached for the knife, but Ayana kicked out, striking Cloe in the jaw and sending her sliding to the other side of the elevator car. Trying to get her body to respond after experiencing so much abuse, Ayana crawled toward the knife, and once she wrapped her hand around the handle, she stumbled to her feet and pointed it at Cloe.

"Where's my son, bitch?"

Giggling, Cloe responded, "You're a much better fighter than your husband."

Shrugging, Ayana stood over Cloe and responded, "Not really. A man with a conscience trained my husband. A monster trained me."

"So was I," Cloe whispered and swept Ayana's feet from under her. Ayana's back hit the floor, pushing all the air out of her lungs and the knife out of her hand. Cloe quickly grabbed the blade, snatched Ayana by the throat, and lifted her to her feet.

"Nice try, bitch, but I fucked you again. Now, get off the elevator, and if you try anything else, whatever I do to you, I'll also do to your sweet little Timothy."

"Okay, okay, just please don't hurt my baby."

"Well, that's entirely up to you and what you're willing to sacrifice for his safety. Now, move."

Ayana walked out of the elevator with Cloe directly behind her, the knife's tip pointed in the back of her neck.

"Stop. We're here. Now knock on the door and make sure your face can be seen through the peephole."

Ayana did what Cloe instructed, and within seconds, the door to the room opened, and Ayana nearly screamed when she looked into the eyes of Thomas Bossa, who appeared highly satisfied with himself. Cloe pushed Ayana inside the room, and as she walked past Thomas, Ayana gave him a look laced with murderous intentions.

"I knew you were a puppet, but I had no idea you were a fucking rat too."

Chuckling, Thomas responded, "I'm just a pawn in a much-larger game. Now, shut the fuck up and have a seat next to the doctor."

When Ayana walked into the living area of the massive suite, she saw Timothy sitting on the couch with two armed guards flanking either side of him. Timothy's eyes widened when he saw Ayana walk into the room, and his entire body went cold with fear.

"Why is she here?" Timothy yelled at Cloe.

"Patience, Doctor. All will be revealed in a moment."

Ayana sat down next to Timothy, placed her head on his shoulder, and whispered in his ear, "My baby is alive."

"I know," he responded while keeping his eyes on Cloe and Thomas, who seemed to be busy watching the screen on a table in the dining area. Cloe had hacked into all the hotel's security camera feeds, and she and Thomas seemed to be looking or waiting for someone to arrive at the hotel.

Ayana lifted her head and looked at Timothy with shock in her eyes.

"Hey, I just found out too."

"What do they want, Tim?"

"If I'm here, you're here, and they have your son as a bargaining chip, I would go out on a limb and say, my vaccine."

"What?"

"Yep, so we are faced with saving the world or saving my godson."

Ayana looked Timothy in his eyes, searching for an answer, and without hesitation, he responded, "I will choose Timmy every time. Don't worry. They can have it. Too many people have suffered for it. I thought it would be a blessing, but I'm discovering it's not a blessing. It's a curse. My curse, and I need to deal with it."

Suddenly, Cloe turned around and said to one of the guards, "Go open the door. They're here."

The guard rushed to the door, and after a few seconds, Maximillian Karlov strolled into the living area, smiling as if he'd just won the lottery.

"You! You son of a bitch. But why? Why put up all that money only to sabotage it?"

Waving him off, Maximillian strolled over to the table where Cloe and Thomas were standing, still watching the camera feeds. Ayana could hear the guard talking to someone else in the foyer, but she couldn't believe her ears as she realized who that person was.

No. No. No. It can't be. It just can't be.

The guard walked back into the room with Patrick Djeng directly behind him, adjusting his black tuxedo jacket. Timothy wasn't surprised to see Patrick walk into the room, but Ayana was devastated, and she leaned over from the sickening knot that throbbed in her stomach. Patrick looked over at her and Timothy and flashed a smile so sinister, they both turned away. The guard was still escorting Patrick toward the table when Patrick told the guard to give him a minute. Bouncing his shoulders, Patrick strolled over toward Timothy and Ayana and sat down on the coffee table in front of them. Clearing his throat to get Ayana's attention, he said, "I would say I'm sorry things came to this, but I would be lying. I'm actually impressed by how all of this worked out, even after the massive fuck-up at your mansion."

Looking up at Patrick, Ayana said, "So it was *you* who ordered the hit on us and sent that bitch to my house to fuck my husband?"

Appearing uncomfortable, Patrick adjusted his collar and responded, speaking loud enough so everyone in the room could hear him, "No, especially the part about fucking your husband. We all work for the same people, and *they* ordered the hit on your family. They came to me and offered me the presidency if I played their game. I've never been a second-place kind of man, especially to a dreamer like Ibrahim. He was too stupid and loved his people too much to be allowed to continue to run my country."

"*Your* country?"

"Yes. It's mines, and as soon as you drop out of the race for 'personal' reasons, Thomas and I will sign the deals that will make both of us insanely rich and powerful."

"So Asim was right about you. That's why he tried to stop you."

"Fuck that relic. He's the past. I'm the future. It's a shame you didn't kill him that day. It would've really helped, but his days are numbered anyway."

"I can't believe you murdered Ibrahim, your friend."

"Actually, I didn't kill Ibrahim. Cloe did the dirty deed. What you people don't realize is that friendships, love, and family will get you killed in this world. Look at all of you, easily manipulated because of your loyalty to one another. You think it makes you stronger, but it makes you an easy target."

"But why would you have me run with you?"

"Because the people love you, and I needed that love to get me the majority vote. Now that I have that, and Thomas has the remaining vote, we'll join forces and win the election automatically once you drop out because we have no opposition. After that, we'll sign the agreements that will make us an exorbitant amount of money."

From behind him, the large frame of Maximillian appeared, and his deep rumbling voice filled their ears when he placed his large hand on Patrick's shoulder and said, "Patrick, you talk too fucking much. You're needed at the table. I need to explain what's expected from the doctor tonight and going forward, and what's at stake if he doesn't comply." Ayana's eyes widened as she watched the president of an entire country obey Maximillian like a loyal puppy without protest.

Maximillian remained standing as he handed Timothy a document that required a signature.

"Read it."

Timothy looked up at the billionaire and then down at the document. After a minute, Timothy started to shake his head while slamming his fist down on the pillows of the couch.

"Why would you want this?"

"Because many people want to make a lot of money while controlling supply and demand. If your vaccine remains as it is, eventually, the trillions of dollars invested in cancer treatment will become obsolete. But if we modify your vaccine to only work for thirty-day intervals, we could, well, not *we,* as if *you'll* be included, but we would make more money than the banks can hold. Just think how much we could charge for each dosage every thirty days for the rest of people's lives. We would rule this fucking planet and not have to hide in the shadows any longer."

"We, as in 'Father'? You are their puppet too?"

"Ha, no, boy. I am one of the puppet masters. All these people in this room work for my partners and me. The ramifications of your vaccine getting out without being under our control were too devastating to leave this in the hands of anyone else."

"And what if I don't sign it?"

"I'm sure you know exactly what's going to happen to that sweet little godson of yours. Cloe is a killer and a psychopath. I'm sure you diagnosed her as soon as the real Cloe surfaced. Unlike John, she doesn't have any reservations about killing children. Shame about John. He was our best operative. It's gonna be hard to replace him, but Cloe is a satisfactory replacement."

"I wouldn't bet on that. I kicked her ass in the elevator, and if I can do that, no telling who else out there can."

"As I said, a 'satisfactory' replacement," Maximillian responded, rolling his eyes and looking back at Cloe in disappointment.

"Okay, fine, I'll sign it."

"Wait, not here, Doctor. During your speech at the ball, you will make your decision public and call me up to the stage and hand me the document. I know you worked hard on writing your acceptance speech, but we have a better one for you. It will explain your decision to turn over the vaccine to the pharmaceutical industry, namely Karlov Pharmaceuticals."

"You son of a bitch. I should kill you."

"You could try, but remember, I'm the former wrestling champion of the world. So, it might not be as easy as you think."

"Fuck you," Timothy snapped while spitting on the rug next to Maximillian's shoe. "I need to take a piss."

"Be my guest. Just make sure you don't lock the door. And if you try anything, we may not be able to kill Mrs. Bennett just yet, but we can make her suffer . . . greatly."

Timothy got up from the couch, but Ayana grasped his arm, stopping him from rising. Patting her hand, he said, "It's okay, Ayana. I'll be right back."

He walked into the bathroom with Maximillian watching him with hatred-filled eyes. Inside the bathroom, Timothy walked in a rage, swinging wildly while crying silent tears of anger. Exhausted from fear and anger, he leaned on the countertop of the sink and looked at himself in the mirror, hating the reflection that stared back at him. Suddenly, the bathroom door opened, and in marched Maximillian. Timothy quickly turned on the faucet and threw water on his face to hide the glistening tears on his cheeks.

"Doctor Avers, are you fucking my wife?"

Hell to da muthafuckin' and two nawls. You hear this nigga? He's not gonna even warm up into it, Timothy thought to himself while he started to wash his hand frantically. Looking at Maximillian through his reflection in the mirror, Timothy responded, "I'm actually washing my hands at the moment."

"Only a coward would refuse to answer a man about fucking his wife."

Timothy shook his head, turned off the water, and walked directly into Maximillian's chest, stared him in his eyes.

"I'm no coward. I just don't respect you enough to tell you the truth. Now, if you don't mind, I'd like to leave, unless you're gonna double-check to see if I shook it well enough?"

"I eat men like you for lunch. You're nothing to me."

"Yeah, I'm sure you do, wrestling half-naked, sweaty men. I'm just not involved in that kind of lifestyle. No judgment, but it's just not my kind of tea bag."

Without warning, Maximillian tried to grapple Timothy, but Timothy grabbed his wrist and, with a swift kick to his knees and the twist of his arm, brought the giant to his knees. Grimacing in pain, Maximillian grunted, "Let me go, or your friend's wife is dead."

Leaning down, Timothy whispered into Maximillian's ear, "I know why you're always in Russia, and it has nothing to do with business. I was curious about why you were so ecstatic when you saw the results of my vaccine. It went well beyond the joy of greed, so I did some digging. I know about your illegitimate 5-year-old daughter and her diagnosis of brain cancer. What I don't understand is why you would risk her life by doing this? I know you love her; I know you want her to live a normal life, but if you let your partners have their way, she *will* die."

Maximillian's body suddenly went limp as he allowed himself to fall to the floor. Sitting up, he looked at Timothy, confused. "Why would you want to help me after everything I've done?"

"I'm not helping you. I'm helping that little girl who has no idea the monster her father is. She's not to blame for who you are. Help me, and in doing so, I'll guarantee she'll receive a dosage from the first batch that goes live—but the unmodified batch."

Maximillian looked down at the floor and then up at Timothy and shook his head in shame. "They are going to kill me if I help you."

"Better you than her, right?"

Nodding, Maximillian gestured for Timothy to help him up, but Timothy looked at his hand as if it were covered in feces.

"Don't push it, Max. You can get your own big ass up off that floor."

Chuckling, Maximillian got off the floor and whispered, "If you betray me, Doctor, I will kill you and everyone you love. My daughter better get that vaccine as soon as humanly possible."

"You have my word."

"How did you find out about her?"

"I'm a genius, Mr. Karlov. I'm supposed to know. If I didn't, I wouldn't be a genius."

"I had no idea you had combat training."

"I took a few classes until I was kicked out."

"Why?"

Timothy was about to tell the billionaire the truth about why he was ejected from Lieutenant Ruiz's training class. Then he remembered how it would shed light on certain things concerning his habit of sleeping with other men's women and decided against it.

"Politics."

Chuckling, Maximillian nodded, and the two men walked out of the bathroom with solemn looks on their faces. Timothy joined Ayana on the couch and gave her hand a reassuring squeeze. Maximillian returned to the table with Cloe, Patrick, and Thomas, and once he got there, Cloe said excitedly, "There he is. He just arrived. I'm going down to deal with him."

Ayana's face went cold as she asked, "Deal with whom?"

Cloe was walking toward the door, securing the silencer on her gun, when she stopped and responded, "Your estranged husband. He's an uncontrollable variable in Father's plan. If he's allowed to live, he could expose the true nature of the original vaccine."

Ayana's eyes began to fill with tears as Timothy searched Maximillian's for answers. The billionaire looked away, letting Timothy know the situation was currently out of his control. He was already signing his own death warrant, but once he aligned himself with Timothy, he was giving away his power to control the situation, and he needed to wait until Timothy gave his speech to switch sides.

"Please don't kill him," Ayana begged while getting on her knees.

"Humph, *now* you cherish him? You spent the last year ignoring him and driving him away from you. *Now* you love him? He almost got beat to death for you, spent countless hours training to protect you, and now you see? *Now* you understand? Too late, stupid bitch. Save your begging for your baby boy because I still have more for you to do. Things that will have you questioning if your son's life is worth the sacrifice. So get off your knees and man up, bitch."

Shaking her head at Ayana like a pitiful pet, Cloe stormed out of the hotel room, leaving Ayana distraught and weeping on her knees.

Daniel strolled through the hotel lobby toward the ballroom, seemingly oblivious to the shadow of death that tailed him. He flowed through the crowded lobby like water, avoiding brushing shoulders with anyone as he made his way toward the men's room. Cloe admired how the black tuxedo hugged his athletic frame, his well-groomed beard, and hair, accenting a near-flaw-less-looking man.

What a waste, Cloe thought, as she turned down the hall toward the men's room. Daniel paused outside the bathroom door to look in the mirror and adjust his bow tie. Cloe stopped and hid behind a corner, carefully observing him while running her fingers seductively over the silencer on her handgun. Eventually, Daniel walked into the men's room, and Cloe quickly followed him inside with her gun raised, ready to fire.

Twenty minutes later, a knock on the door echoed through the hotel room, and one of the armed guards rushed to the door. Looking through the peephole, he could see Cloe staring back at him, her eyes blue and careless.

"It's Cloe. She's back," the guard announced as he opened the door. Hearing the guard say that could only mean one thing, and Ayana buried her head in Timothy's shoulder. Timothy fought back the tears, trying to accept his friend was dead. The guard opened the door, and a sudden bullet to the throat sent him flying backward into the hotel room's foyer. His body slid on the tiled floor until it was visible in the living area. Timothy tightened his embrace on Ayana as the other two guards cautiously moved closer to the foyer.

"Sorry to crash the party, but I couldn't resist a good time."

John's familiar Scottish accent came from behind the guards, and as they all turned around, John planted several bullets in their skulls. The sound of the guards' bodies hitting the floor startled Patrick, and when he saw John walking toward them, he screamed, "How did you get in here?"

Tilting his head to the side while his eyelids lowered halfway over his eyes, John annoyingly responded, "Why does everyone ask me that, as if they don't know what I'm capable of?"

Slowly, Daniel walked into the living area from the foyer, with his arm wrapped around Cloe's neck and her own gun pressed against her temple. Ayana screamed with joy and jumped up from the couch, but John motioned for her to stay put as the two armed men closed in on Patrick, Thomas, and Maximillian.

"Now, who's going to tell me where my son is?"

No one said a word, so Daniel fired a shot into Thomas's kneecap, sending him reeling and screaming to the floor. John glanced over at Daniel with a look of pride and then returned his attention to their adversaries.

"I won't ask again. The next bullet is for your legs, *Mr. President.*"

"You wouldn't dare. I am a head of state."

"I don't give a fuck who you are. I want my son. Where is he?"

Accepting Daniel meant business, Patrick responded, "Only she knows where your son is."

"Well, that's unfortunate because I'm sure she's not gonna talk."

"You fucking right, and after tonight, you can have the unique privilege of burying your son twice, you stupid son of a bi—"

Daniel pulled the trigger, sending a bullet straight through Cloe's temple and splattering blood and brain matter all over Patrick's face.

"What the fuck?" Patrick screamed as he tried to spit Cloe's bloody brains out of his mouth. Cloe's eyes rolled into her head as her lifeless body dropped to the floor. Daniel aimed his weapon and continued to shoot into her body until his clip was empty. Exhaling as if he'd just drunk a refreshing glass of water, he reached into his jacket pocket, reloaded, and aimed his gun at Patrick.

"Now that we understand each other, where is my son?"

"He's here in Chicago. She always keeps him close."

"I don't have time for games, Mr. President. Chicago is a big city. I need an address—now."

While Patrick screamed out the address, Timothy yelled, "How did you know? How did you know he knew where Timothy was?"

"I didn't, but hearing her threaten Timothy after everything she's done to us just rubbed me the wrong way," Daniel responded, shrugging his shoulders.

Daniel's coy demeanor was eerily familiar, and when Ayana noticed John's look of pride at Daniel's response, she gasped in horror.

"You've been training Danny?"

John's smile widened as he replied, "That's right, and it's beautiful. A chip off the old block, don't you agree?"

Looking at the three men in front of him, Daniel asked, "So what shall we do with you?"

"Danny, wait. Maximillian is with us now. We need him, but Patrick and Thomas, you can toss those two muthafuckas out the window for all I care."

Two evil grins grew on Daniel's and John's faces as they looked at Patrick and Thomas and then at the balcony to their right.

"As much as I want to see these two pay for everything they have done, we can't throw them out of the window and not have an international incident," Ayana warned as she walked over to Daniel's side. Leaning against him and perching her chin on his shoulder, she looked down at Cloe's body on the floor and smiled like a child standing in front of a fully stacked Christmas tree. Timothy felt sick to his stomach as he watched Ayana and Daniel's satisfied expressions while they both reveled in Cloe's body bleeding out on the floor.

These two shouldn't be with anyone else other than each other. Demented muthafuckas.

John looked over at Ayana and Daniel and swallowed hard as he tried to subdue his jealousy. As beads of liquid envy appeared on his forehead, a small voice inside screamed for him to aim his weapon at Daniel and take him out of the equation, but he knew that might not go over well with Ayana. Lowering his gun and reaching into his back pocket, he pulled out a digital recorder. He started playing back Patrick's entire conversation with Ayana and Timothy, including his confession of assassinating Ibrahim Alraheem.

"Looks like Father is gonna have to find another set of puppets because you two are getting executed," John said, laughing while waving the recorder in Patrick's face. "I hate to break up the reunion, but you all have a party to attend. I'll clean up this and make sure these two are handed over to the proper people, and then I'll go get your baby boy and bring him to you."

Ayana immediately began to protest another assassin handling her son, but Daniel stopped her and said, "John will bring him to us. Relax and trust me."

Ayana looked into Daniel's eyes and saw a confidence and calm she hadn't seen in years. His spirit began to give her faith in his word, and she slowly nodded in agreement.

"This is all very touching, but you have to leave unless you want to explain this to the Secret Service. Oh, by the way, Doctor Bennett," John sniffed, "no father could ever be as proud as I am right now. Enjoy the party and be home by midnight," John said, pretending he was going to cry.

What kind of gay Niggarella shit are these two on? Timothy thought as he walked toward the front door with Maximillian beside him. Before Timothy left the room, he turned to John and said, "Thank you for saving our lives."

John gave him a chilling look and coldly responded, "Don't thank me for this or anything—you most of all. Don't ever thank me for anything."

Feeling a sudden cold draft blow over him, Timothy quickly walked out of the suite.

An hour later, in a packed ballroom filled with some of the most powerful and influential people in the world, Timothy accepted an award from the president of the United States and announced the real benefits of his vaccine. Maximillian Karlov joined Timothy on the stage, moved to tears as he understood what this announcement meant for him and his daughter. Daniel was present with Ayana seated next to him, appearing to be attentively watching the celebration, but his mind was traveling through time, back to three months ago, when he had the most unlikely and unwelcome visitor to his new downtown condo.

Chapter Twenty

Belle of the Ball

Three months prior
Chicago, Illinois

The sudden movement of his mattress surprised Daniel out of his sleep, and he quickly reached behind his head under his pillow for his gun. As his hands frantically searched for his weapon, he soon discovered there was nothing there but air. Someone was sitting on the edge of his bed, staring at him like a rat in a maze. Sitting up, Daniel moved toward the other side of the bed while the man just sat there in silence.

"I see you're scared, and you should be because I'm still trying to convince myself not to kill you."

"John? What the fuck are you doing in my house?"

"Trying to convince myself not to kill you, that's what. Are you deaf or still asleep?"

"So, I take it your employer forgave you for not following orders?"

"Hmm, not sure, actually. But I have been given a chance to redeem myself . . . of sorts."

"By murdering me?"

"Murder? Lord, no. Murder is such a personal word, which should be used for those who are too helpless to defend themselves. You are not helpless, good Doctor. You are more than capable of defending yourself, so if I decide to take your life, it would be a righteous kill. Not murder."

"So, you *are* here for me."

"Not to kill you, although I want to for my own selfish and outlandish reasons."

"You are in love with my wife. I can't believe this shit."

"Love? I wouldn't say, love. Maybe a strong like. Well, 'strong' is too weak of a word. Let's say I'm whatever it is between insanity and love. Yeah, that's me."

"Stupid?"

"Indeed. Anyway, I've decided."

"Wait, whoa," Daniel yelled, holding up his hands as John reached out to him with a gun in his hands.

"Calm down, princess. I've decided not to kill you. Here's your weapon back. Jeez, nervous much?"

Daniel snatched the gun, removed the safety, and pulled the trigger, but nothing happened.

"Oh, I removed the firing pin while you were sleeping. So, I guess I'm not as stupid as you believe."

"What the fuck?"

"Let's shed some light on the situation, shall we?"

Suddenly, Daniel's nightstand lamp came on, pushing back the darkness and revealing the worried look on John's face. Daniel had never seen the assassin so unsure of himself. He was almost . . . frightened.

"John, what's going on?"

"Well, my good Doctor, it appears a very sinister plot is being weaved at you and your family's expense, and I can't foil it alone. I need help—*your* help."

"How can *I* help you?"

"Well, I need you to help me kill people. But in the name of justice, of course."

"Of course."

"Let me tell you all about it, and then you decide if you're in, okay?"

Over the next three hours, John briefed Daniel about Cloe, his son, and the plot to steal Timothy's vaccine. As John concluded his briefing, Daniel became furious, storming around his bedroom like a Viking, absorbed with bloodlust.

"Those motherfuckers. They destroyed my marriage, kidnapped my son, and ruined my life."

"Well, in their defense, *you* helped ruin your marriage. Although you were faithful to your lovely wife, you weren't honest, and Cloe used it against you."

"And that fucking nerve cream."

"Oh, yes, that. Nasty business, isn't it? I mean, it's already bad enough she has really great . . . you know, but to enhance the sensation with an ointment, now, *that's* unforgivable."

"Wait a fucking minute. How do you know how great it is?"

"Well, in Africa when she was at your place, she and I may have . . . well, that's not important. What's important is, are you in?"

This motherfucker fucked this bitch right under our noses. I can't believe this asshole.

"Why are you looking at me like that, Doctor? Hey, sharing is caring, right?"

Shaking his head, Daniel responded, "Whatever. Of course, I'm in, but my training won't be enough to fight Cloe. Especially if she's as good as you say she is."

"I didn't say she was good. I said 'satisfactory' as a replacement once my time to retire draws nearer."

"Satisfactory or great, my training isn't enough."

"And that's why I'm here, good man. I will train you."

"We have three months before the banquet. You've been an assassin for years. I can't see three months making much of a difference."

"I beg to differ. You already have weapons and tactic training, so you're halfway there. All you need now is the killer instinct and a few more crucial elements added to your hand-to-hand combat. Well, maybe more than a few, but if you follow my lead and apply yourself, I can assure you that you will be more than equipped to handle any adversary."

Daniel paced around his bedroom, trying to decide if he should trust the assassin again after he nearly beat him to death while secretly coveting his wife.

"Why should I trust you?"

"You shouldn't, but you *should* trust if you don't help me, your son, wife, and friend will perish."

"Okay, I'm in. I know I'm gonna regret this."

"Absolutely, but once I'm done with you, in three months, you'll be the belle of the ball."

"Has anyone told you you're an assho—"

"Yes, constantly. You should embrace it as I do."

The next three months, John enslaved Daniel's body and mind, training him in the rigorous trade of clandestine murder and espionage. During their training, he also instructed Daniel to behave like a man who's given up on life. Then no one would view him as a threat. Otherwise, Father would send someone to deal with the threat before they could stop the impending disaster. During the three months of preparation, the two men observed the Hyatt and planted listening devices all over the hotel to get any inside information they could use.

Several days before the banquet, John snuck into the suite and hid between the walls until the night of the banquet with a listening device to record all conversations. Daniel was supposed to wait until Ayana and Timothy had been brought to the suite the evening of the banquet, and all players involved were present. The wait was torture because Daniel feared their plan wouldn't work, and his wife, son, and best friend would be killed—especially if Timothy decided not to turn over the vaccine.

As Cloe followed him through the noisy and crowded lobby, Daniel could sense her, smell her, even single out her breathing from the hundreds of people around him without much effort. It was at that moment he understood just how effective John's training was over Ruiz's Navy SEAL training. He'd been timing her footsteps to see how much time he had from the corner where she was hiding until she reached the bathroom door. When she walked into the bathroom, Cloe looked around and noticed he wasn't at any of the urinals or in the stalls. She saw that the bathroom had no windows for him to escape, and the heating and cooling vents were too small for an escape route. At that moment, she looked up and saw Daniel bracing himself on the wall over the door, to her right.

Kicking her in the face, Daniel jumped down, and when Cloe swung her gun in his direction, he ducked under her arm and struck her in the pressure point between her armpit and ribs. Her hand involuntarily released the weapon, sending it clattering to the floor. Cloe hesitated, expecting Daniel to go for the gun, but he knew he didn't need it. Cloe looked at him, confused by his lack of interest in the weapon, and during her distraction, he hit her with a skull-jarring right hook, knocking her unconscious. Daniel was standing over her when she came to, pointing her gun at her head with a satisfying smile on his face. Looking up at him, confused and bewildered, Cloe asked, "Who trained you?"

Chuckling, he responded, "The fact you had to ask is disappointing."

Now, sitting next to his wife at the banquet while they held hands, Daniel considered everything and everyone he had to go through just for the privilege to touch her again.

Totally worth it.

Watching his friend give hope to the world should've been moving for him, but Daniel had experienced the darkest side of humanity, and although this vaccine would be a much-needed light, he knew someone would fight to diminish it. Ayana held his hand and noticed her palms were sweating, and that tingly feeling down her spine returned. Closing her eyes and inhaling deeply, she tried to calm her anxiety about something happening that would prevent John from returning her baby to her. Simply put, she knew she had to trust her husband, who just so happened to be a total badass now. Glancing over at him, she noticed something missing in his eyes. He'd seen and experienced so much that it changed him. She just hoped the change wouldn't make it more difficult for the two of them to love each other again. Ayana couldn't deny she still harbored a great amount of anger toward her husband, and it would take some time for them to reconcile, but she was willing to do the work if he were. Also, watching him empty his clip in Cloe was definitely a great start on the road to reconciliation.

Fucking loved every single bullet he put in her. I almost came watching that bitch die.

After dinner, Daniel received a message from John to head home, and although the party was just beginning, the tortured parents wanted to be elsewhere. The ride to Daniel's condo was silent and tense, as neither of them wanted to say anything that could ruin an already intense yet long overdue reunion. When Daniel turned the doorknob to his condo and heard the small pitter-patter of running feet toward the door, the parents immediately burst into tears. Li'l Timothy was frail and weak from being underfed by his captor, but his excitement gave him the strength to jump into their arms. The three of them collapsed on the floor in the foyer, hugging and weeping loudly. Daniel's entire body shook as he grasped his family as if letting them go would cause them to vanish into thin air. He'd put it all on the line, trusting a man who was once his enemy and wanted what he had to help bring his family back to him.

He gambled big, and the payoff was divine, and at that moment, nothing else mattered. John watched the family's emotional reunion and smiled. Nodding, he finally accepted his rightful place in this symphony and slowly backed away, disappearing into the darkness.

A few hours later, Ayana sat on the couch next to Li'l Timothy and ran her fingers through his hair as he slept. Daniel watched her, smiling, but he didn't want to disturb her, so he started to walk away. Ayana reached out, grabbed his hand, and shook her head.

Standing up, she looked him in his eyes, and tears erupted. Without warning, her right hand flew through the air, slapping him across the face. Daniel stood deathly still as he continued to stare into her eyes. Her left hand came next, smacking him across the face, again, yet Daniel appeared unaffected by her physical aggression. Ayana struck him on his face and pounded on his chest as she cried out in anger and pain. She continued her assault until she could barely stand, eventually leaned forward, and rested her head on his chest. Daniel held her in his arms and whispered in her ear, "I'm sorry for not being the husband and man you deserve. I have no excuse for my actions. I don't deserve a second chance, but I pray you will still give it to me."

Ayana looked him in his eyes and kissed him softly on his lips. The softness of her lips, the yearning of wanting to feel her kiss him again, felt like nirvana. Grateful and excited, he held her head in his hands and kissed her passionately. Ayana jumped into his arms and gasped, "Fuck me, please. I want you to fuck me."

Refusing to leave their son alone, Daniel carried Ayana over to the armchair, turned her around, and bent her over the armrest. Pulling her long evening dress up, he reached under and violently ripped her panties off. Ayana gasped as she felt Daniel's lips and tongue exploring her. He ate her passionately and violently, devouring her like a starving predator. Ayana bit down on the chair's fabric to contain her squeals of pleasure as Daniel brought her to climax repeatedly with his mouth. Sweating and feeling faint, she started to stand up, but Daniel wasn't finished. A hard, deep thrust inside of her caused her eyes to open wide as she howled loudly from the pain and pleasure. Gripping her amazing hips, Daniel braced himself and began to stroke his wife with the longing of a man desperate to reconnect with the love of his life. Ayana closed her eyes and whispered, "I love you so much," as his incredible agony sent her to ecstasy.

Chapter Twenty-One

The Decision

The morning after the award banquet
Chicago, Illinois

Timothy sat up with a burning headache from the festivities of the night before and looked around his condo as if he were a stranger to his surroundings. Reaching for the remote, he turned on the wall-mounted, curved OLED, and the red scroll of breaking news began rolling across the bottom of the screen. His eyes nearly popped out of his head as he read the headline:

Billionaire Maximillian Karlov commits suicide, confesses to pedophilia, and child prostitution in a suicide letter written to wife, Simone Karlov.

Timothy suddenly felt sick to his stomach. He ran into the bathroom to unleash the food and alcohol from the night before. After gathering himself, taking a shower, and dressing, he rushed out the front door to Simone. On his way to her house, he began to reflect on his life and the countless choices he's made. Friendships, family, and relationships all started to play back in his memory like a tragic comedy reel of good times and bad decisions. It soon became painfully apparent that after all his carnal connections, he realized he had no one to leave his massive fortune and copyrights to should anything happen to him. After being brought close to tears from the revelation, he decided that he would be heading downtown to speak to his lawyer after leaving Simone's South Barrington mansion.

Two weeks after Maximillian's funeral, Timothy decided to stop by Daniel and Ayana's new mansion in Lake Forest's northern suburb. He really missed them, and after watching Simone mourn the loss of her husband, he longed for their company. When he walked through the door, the feeling of happiness and family hit him like a ray of sunshine. Li'l Timmy was running through the house as he used to before all the madness started, and the sight of his smile melted Timothy's heart instantly. Joining his friends in the kitchen, Timothy watched the married couple interact with each other. He could feel a renewed love between them, and he secretly longed for the same with Simone.

After all these two have been through, they still managed to stay together and stay in love. I can't hope to have their kind of love, but if Simone and I can have just half of their magic, that would be more than enough for me.

Timothy hung out with his friends and godson until he received a text message from Simone, asking him to come over immediately. Daniel noticed the boyish grin on his face while he read his text message and rolled his eyes.

"You gotta go, don't you?"

"Yeah, sorry, guys."

"No worries, 'widow whacker.'"

"Oh no, no, you didn't just go there."

Shrugging, Daniel smiled, took another sip of wine, and walked out of the kitchen.

"Don't pay him any mind, Tim. I'm happy for you. Go see your woman. We'll see you next week for Christmas, right?"

"Absolutely. I wouldn't miss it for the world. Just make sure you make room for my plus ten."

"Plus ten? You bringing a BBW?" Daniel yelled from the family room.

Timothy's eyelids lowered over his eyes as he shook his head and said, "It's like a piece of him is still here."

"Who?"

"John."

Giggling, Ayana responded, "Yeah, I know, but it's also refreshing to see him with a sense of humor, even if it's really dark at times."

"I guess. Anyway, I'm outta here."

"Not before you give me my goodbye hug and kiss," Li'l Timothy's tiny voice said from behind his godfather. Timothy's face lit up as he turned around and snatched him in the air, wrapped him in his arms, and kissed him on the cheek.

"I love you, Timmy. Don't you ever forget that Uncle Timothy loves you."

"I know you do. Just make sure next time you come over, you bring candy."

"So, I can't come empty-handed?"

"Nope."

"Deal."

Later that night, Timothy walked into Simone's Hyde Park townhouse, expecting the usual, but tonight, she met him at the door in all-black lingerie and led him into her bedroom. Her master suite was lit up with candles, and soft music flowed through the air like invisible silk. Timothy's eyes sparkled as she slowly led him to the bed and whispered, "Make love to me."

Simone had never before been this way with him, and the idea of them sharing more than sex excited more than his carnal side. Kissing her softly on the lips, Timothy laid her down on the bed and began to make love to her. The connection between them grew stronger with each sensual stroke, touch, taste, and climax. Electrical charges of emotions sparked each time their naked skin touched, jump-starting a love they both lost years ago. Their desires translated through their flesh, and without saying a word, they brought unbridled pleasure to each other. It was the most amazing sex he'd ever had, and when they were done, and Simone placed her head on his chest, Timothy knew there was no other love he'd dedicate himself to.

Running her fingers along his stomach muscles, Simone whispered, "It's too soon, I know, but I was wondering if one day you would consider—"

"Yes, yes, yes."

"You haven't even heard the question."

"Doesn't matter. Whatever you want, the answer is yes."

Simone looked up at him and smiled.

"So, you really want to be with me? Despite everything I've done to you, and what I may do to you?"

"Yes, I do."

"Even knowing how you and I got back together by cheating on my dead husband?"

The reminder made Timothy slightly uncomfortable, and he cleared his throat while adjusting his back on the pillow.

"Yes, even still."

"Even when I tell you, I murdered my husband, and I work for the same people that tried to steal your vaccine and kill your friends?"

Timothy's heart froze in his chest as her words cut him deeply. Trembling, he slowly sat up and looked in her eyes for answers. Simone sat up and looked Timothy in his eyes with deep sorrow and regret.

"I hate for you to find out this way, but if you and I are to be husband and wife, you need to know everything and accept it."

"Accept it?"

"Yes, Father is impressed by your resilience and would like for you to take the place of my late husband as a council member. Imagine the power you and I would have. Paired with your vaccine, you could rise to be the Grandfather."

"Grandfather?"

"Yes, the head of it all. The one who everyone answers to. Presidents, corporations, warlords, armies . . . Every powerful and influential person would answer to you, my love. Can you imagine it?"

Timothy remained silent as his heart shattered to pieces in his chest. As Simone seductively continued to convince him, he started to put together every interaction between them. Everything she'd done was to recruit him, and now that her husband was out of the way, he was her next assignment.

"But why did you have to kill him?"

"Because he betrayed Father, and I was given the task of ending his life."

"So, the suicide letter was all bullshit?"

"Yes. Father doesn't just take your life. He also takes your legacy."

"So, you're an assassin too?"

"God, no. I'm a whore."

"What?"

"Well, I started as one. I was *their* whore, fucking whomever they said needed fucking to convince them of something. When I left college and was pregnant with your child, I was in a bad place, and that's when they recruited me. They wanted Mr. Karlov to join them because of his connections to weapons and other off-the-books commodities. So, they sent me to fuck him into submission."

"Did he know? Did he know who and what you were?"

"Not at first, but when I presented him with the invitation, I told him everything."

"And he still married you?"

"Are you still considering marrying me, even after everything I just told you?"

Timothy looked away, refusing to answer her question.

"Exactly."

"So, all of this had nothing to do with love?"

"Babe, love? Listen, I gave up on love a long time ago and settled for power instead. Love will get you killed. Love will leave you broke and betrayed. I care for you, Timothy, more than I actually should, but I can't honestly say I love you and mean it."

"Then what the fuck is it all for?"

"Power."

"Not enough for me."

"Listen, Timothy, join us, be with me, and let's rule the world together."

"What's the catch?"

"What do you mean?"

"These motherfuckas aren't going to offer me a seat at their table just because there's an opening. That's never happened to a Black man in the history of the planet. So, what's the fucking catch?"

"You have to modify the vaccine."

Those words were the final nail in the coffin. There was nothing worse than finding out your dream that seemed right at your fingertips was all a lie. That your dream really isn't yours, but a well-played out charade, by a woman that had the rhythm of your heart. No other woman had moved his soul the way Simone did, and no other woman broke him down more than she did. Shaking his head while trying to contain his emotions, Timothy responded, "Goodbye, Simone."

Simone watched him climb out of her bed, kiss her gently on the lips, and leave. As the sound of her front door closing echoed through the lonely townhome, she felt a salty lump grow in her throat. Suddenly, her eyes started to burn as they released rivers of regret down her face. She wept alone on her bed, not quite able to get the sound of his voice out of her head. The sound of forever in his tone kept poisoning her like liquid mercury. As the two words kept repeating in her head, she rocked back and forth on her bed, trying her best to convince herself she was telling the truth when she said she didn't really love him.

Chapter Twenty-Two

Merry Christmas

The mansion was teeming with life and celebration as the sounds of laughter and toasting glasses filled the air. It was a full house, with the men ruling the family room and the women ruling the kitchen. As usual, Daniel's mother was the general as she stood in the middle of the kitchen, whipping a large bowl of mashed potatoes by hand. Ayana, Meagan, and Daniel's sisters watched her in admiration, impressed by her strength and the perfect muscle tone of her arms as they spun the whipping tool effortlessly. Noticing their curiosity, she smiled and said, "Take notes, ladies, I make 63 look good."

"No, Mrs. Bennett, you make it look *flawless*," Ayana responded while shaking her head in amazement. The men yelled out from behind her as Daniel's father won another round of chess against Timothy. The men exaggerated every move during the chess game, teasing Timothy every time the older man backed him in a corner. Aggravated yet amused, Timothy got up from the table and walked into the kitchen to grab another beer. He swore loudly when he noticed there weren't anymore, causing Mrs. Bennett to stop whipping the potatoes and flash him a nasty look.

Clearing his throat, Timothy said, "Sorry, Mrs. Bennett."

"Keep it up, Timothy. There's plenty of soap in this house."

The women all laughed hysterically at Timothy's embarrassed shock on his face as her threat took him down memory lane. He was quickly reminded that as a child, she actually *did* wash out his mouth with soap.

"There isn't any more beer?"

"If there isn't any in the cooler, then we're out," Ayana responded.

"I guess a beer run is in order?"

"Looks that way. See if Daniel will go with you," Ayana suggested.

Timothy started walking into the family room but stopped when he noticed Daniel sitting down at the chess table.

There's no way I'm going to pull him from there.

Meagan seeing Daniel sitting down as well, tapped Timothy on the shoulder and said, "I'll go with you."

"Nah, it's okay. I'll go by myself."

"No, Timothy, you shouldn't go by yourself. Plus, we need to talk. It's long overdue."

Seeing there was no convincing her otherwise, Timothy nodded his head and said, "Grab your coat. I'll wait for you at the front door."

Meagan smiled and gleefully pranced toward the coat closet.

Rolling her eyes at her friends, Ayana noticed the kitchen trash bin overflowing, so she pulled it out and carried it outside. The savage bite of the frigid subzero wind chill ripped through her sweater, and without thinking, she swore loudly. Worried that Mrs. Bennett heard her, she paused for a second to listen. Once she was satisfied she was in the clear, she started down the back stairs toward the trash cans.

A shuffling of snow to her right made her jump, and when she turned around, a modest-looking John walked out of the shadows. Dropping the trash bag and holding her hand over her chest, Ayana gasped, "You *really* are an asshole, John."

She became worried when the expected sarcastic response didn't come out of his mouth. Feeling he meant her no harm, yet something was horribly wrong, she walked over to him and asked, "Is everything okay?"

"How's your son?"

Still confused, she responded, "He's fine, but what about you?"

"I'm in a weird place, love, and I don't know how to get out of it."

"Well, why don't you come inside. There's plenty of food and—"

"My time for family gatherings ended decades ago, love. I used to have a family, not as large as your husband's, but it was perfect for me. But in my line of work, love is a liability, and my employers didn't like playing second fiddle to my wife and son. So, they taught me a lesson of loyalty and loss."

Ayana placed her hand over her mouth as a quiet squeal escaped her lips. John smiled at her reaction and said, "It's my fault, really, thinking I could be the man that I am and still have meaningful connections without Karma coming to collect her dues. Cherish your family, especially your husband. He's a good man; a little naïve at times, but definitely a better man than I could ever be."

Becoming increasingly worried, Ayana took a step back and asked, "John, why are you here?"

"I don't know. I shouldn't be here, but I had to say something to you in person, so you'd know I'm sincere."

Suddenly, Timothy's loud voice traveled outside as he yelled, "We'll be right back."

Ayana turned around, and at that moment, John stepped closer to her and whispered in her ear, "I'm terribly sorry."

Startled, Ayana spun back around and asked, "Sorry about wh—"

The explosive blast rocked the entire house as flames and debris flew through the air, crashing through the front windows of the mansion. Ayana fell backward onto the snow. Her eyes widened as she watched a cloud of fire and smoke rise above her home. Looking around, she noticed John was gone, and then she heard Daniel screaming Timothy's name. *Timothy.* Her heart sank in her chest as she cried at the thought that her baby was dead. She jumped up from the ground, bolted through the kitchen door, and raced toward the family room, where her son was before she went outside. Everyone was on the floor, and after searching over the room, she saw his grandfather sheltering her son.

Suddenly, she heard Daniel's screams coming from the house entrance, and she closed her eyes in agony when she finally realized Daniel wasn't screaming her son's name. A vivid memory of a smile flashed in her mind, sweet and angelic. A smile that inspired her for years, a smile that gave her hope and strength, and the last smile she would ever see from her friend again.

Meagan, Meagan, Meagan, Meagan.

At first, Ayana thought she was screaming her friend's name in her head, but as she bolted out the front door and watched Timothy's car burn, she discovered it wasn't just in her mind. Ayana screamed until her throat became dry and raw, and then she pushed her vocal cords until they bled. She screamed until her head exploded in pain, and she screamed like a thousand lost souls being sent to the underworld into the welcoming claws of eternal suffering. She screamed until her body couldn't anymore.

As she walked closer to the burning car, she noticed two bodies still inside, set aflame and lifeless, their mouths agape in terror. Daniel fell to his knees, his soul blown to pieces like Timothy's Mercedes, his soul burning in the pits of hell from the pain of hopelessly watching his best friend burn. Ayana joined him on her knees, and the two of them stared at the burning car as the faraway echoes of sirens traveled through the winter night.

As John walked through the snow and turned around, he watched the flames lick above the tree line surrounding the Bennetts' estate. Out of the hundreds of lives he'd taken, this was by far the most difficult. When Cloe allowed him to view the contract and Timothy's profile appeared on the screen, he knew it would be a tough ride for him. He didn't do it to be free of Father. Death would've been a more welcoming option. No, he did it to save Ayana and her son's life. The African woman and her son reminded him so much of his murdered Ethiopian wife and their son that he had to make a choice . . . and he chose Ayana. He knew killing Timothy and Meagan would make her hate him, and he was all right with that as long as she was alive. Smiling to himself, he reflected on the real reason he trained the doctor as harshly as he did. He knew one day they would face each other again, and he wanted to even the playing field a bit. After killing Daniel's best friend, he felt he owed him that much. Climbing into his Aston Martin, John started the engine, took one last glimpse of the flames, thinking, *Let the chase begin.*

Chapter Twenty-Three

Last Will and Abduction

Weeks . . . that's all Daniel could figure how long it's been since he'd buried his friend. Weeks of mourning, weeks of nightmares, weeks of regret, weeks of guilt, weeks of planning revenge. The world was a different place without Timothy, and the pharmaceutical industry was in turmoil as everyone tried to pirate his vaccine. No one knew how or who had the sequence to replicate it. The only person who had the rights to it was dead, and so far, no one had any idea if he left the priceless vaccine to anyone else in the event of his death. Li'l Timothy absorbed Ayana's grief, and although she would wake up in the middle of the night screaming her friend's name, her night terrors were less frequent than Daniel's.

Drinking in his home office while going through their high school yearbook, Daniel's cell phone began to vibrate. Initially, he'd decided to ignore it, but whoever was calling was annoyingly persistent. So, he snatched up his cell phone and growled, "Stop calling this number."

"I'm afraid I can't do that, Doctor Bennett."

"Who the fuck is this?"

"My name is Michael Gradkowski, Doctor Avers's lawyer."

"Oh, great. You want to know if Timothy left the vaccine's formula with me?"

"Well, actually . . . You know what, Doctor Bennett? It's imperative that I speak to you and your wife immediately."

The urgency and fear in the lawyer's voice aroused Daniel's curiosity, and he figured there were only a few things that would scare a high-profile lawyer like Gradkowski.

"Fine, we will be in your office tomorrow."

"No. I need you here today. In a couple of hours, actually; otherwise, I'm skipping town, Doctor. Some bizarre things are going on around me, and I will not take any chances, especially after what happened to my client."

"Fair enough. We'll be there in two hours."

"Thank you so much, Doctor," the lawyer said, exhaling forcefully.

"Goodbye, Mr. Gradkowski."

Two hours later, Daniel and Ayana arrived at Michael Gradkowski's downtown office, while Daniel's father and brothers waited in the car with Li'l Timothy. They had both decided after they got him back from Cloe that they would never again leave him alone with anyone that wasn't family. As soon as Michael's secretary announced they had arrived, the lawyer rushed out of his office, covered in sweat and the smell of liquor. Ayana's nose turned up when she noticed the wet stains under the armpits of his light blue collared shirt. Daniel stared at the lawyer and shook his head in disgust.

Fucking coward.

Ayana looked over at her husband's facial expression and smiled. Daniel was definitely a different man.

Whatever fear he had before, John trained it out of him, and he was as stern and solid as a tank made of diamonds.

"Please, Dr. and Mrs. Bennett, follow me."

"Don't you think you need a shower first?" Daniel asked, turning up his nose at the ripe smell of funk that emanated from the lawyer's body. Ayana elbowed Daniel in his side and whispered, "Be nice."

The lawyer's odor seemed to thicken once they walked into his office, and he closed the door behind them. Ayana coughed and then took a seat, but Daniel remained standing, looking around at every closed window in his office while tapping his feet on the carpet. The smell was so putrid, Daniel felt like it was attaching itself to him permanently, and he couldn't take it any longer.

"Mike, if you don't get your stank ass up and open up these fucking windows, I will toss your ass out of one of them."

Michael leaped out of his chair and frantically opened every window in his office, allowing the winter air to flow into the office and dilute the smell. After being satisfied that the air was somewhat fit for human breathing, Daniel took a seat and gestured for the lawyer to get on with it.

"I'll be quick. Your friend, my client, left a last will and testament in this video that he had me film, not long before his death." Michael then handed the couple a seven-inch tablet and said, "Press *play*."

Daniel and Ayana looked at each other, and then Daniel pressed the *play* button. Timothy's face appeared on the screen, and Daniel's heart rate began to increase the longer he looked at his friend's image. Timothy flashed his signature smile, displaying his perfect set of teeth, and began to speak.

"Hey, guys, I know it's weird that I'm smiling on the video that would indicate I'm a dead motherfucker, but you know me. I always do weird shit. Seriously, most people give these things a lot of thought, but it was an easy decision for me. Since I lost my parents, you've been my family, and it only made sense to pass on my legacy to you, my family. So, I, Dr. Timothy Avers, being of sound mind and body, hereby pass on my considerable wealth and legacy to my brother from another mother, Dr. Daniel Bennett, Ayana Bennett, and my godson Timothy Bennett."

He paused for a moment, trying to collect his thoughts and gather himself before continuing. "It's strange hearing my name with the Bennett last name behind it, something I dreamed could be a reality my entire life, and who'd have thought my wish was granted. I know that you will do right by this vaccine, and you will make sure it helps the world. I love you, brother, and don't mourn me for too long. Get on with your life. Keep loving on that beautiful wife of yours and enjoy your son. Don't be consumed with hate and regret, brother. I made all these decisions that led me to where I am now, and after careful consideration, I wouldn't change anything besides leaving South Sudan when you needed me the most. For that, I am truly sorry."

Timothy started to move away from the camera, and it looked as if he'd just remembered something. He sat back down and said, "Oh, and by the way, I need you to take care of my son. Yep, that's right. I have a son. Simone didn't abort our baby. She gave him up for adoption. I found him a few weeks ago. He's living in Philadelphia with a great family. Would you know he wants to be a doctor too? Ironic, isn't it? Michael has all of his information. His name is Dorian. A pretty white-ass name for a black-ass baby, but you know Simone and how she is. Find him and tell him who his father really was, tell him . . . just tell him although I'll never get to meet him, I love him. Oh, and one more thing, white bitches are still crazy."

Then laughing hysterically, he moved out of the camera's focus, and the video ended. Tears fell from Daniel's eyes as he tightly gripped the tablet until its plastic casing started to crack and bend. Michael quickly started pulling the tablet out of his hands while saying, "Okay, I think that's quite enough, Doctor Bennett. Let it go. I don't have any other copies of this video. If you destroy it, you'll have no rights to the contents of this briefcase."

The lawyer then handed Daniel a black briefcase that was all too familiar to him.

Timothy, I miss you, brother.

"What's in that briefcase gives you access to Timothy's fortune and his formula that he hid in a secret location. He told me you would understand the clues he left behind. Are we good now?"

"Sure, we're good," Daniel responded while rising to his feet.

"Great. Have fun. I'm leaving town tonight."

"Make sure you wash that funk off before you step on a plane. Your stench is gunmetal hard and might set off some alarms at the checkpoints."

As Ayana and Daniel turned to leave his office, Michael's secretary called the lawyer and told him he had more visitors.

"What? I didn't schedule any—"

When Daniel opened the office door, he was face-to-face with the beautiful and determined Simone Karlov.

"Hello, Doctor. I'm sorry to barge in like this, but Father would like to see both of you, *now*."

The End